THE ROMAN SLAVEGIRL

by

SYRA BOND

I0566646

Published by **CHIMERA**
ISBN 9781780807768

This novel is fiction - in real life practice safe sex.

Preface

After my time with Galen and the others in Spain, I was keen to get away as quickly as I could. Africa was my dream but I could not afford the ferry from Algeciras. Sitting on the dock in despair, I was promised free passage on a cargo ship if I was prepared to work for the crew. However, their idea of 'work' was only a perverted form of slavery. They kept me locked up in a greasy engine room, tying me by the wrists to pipe and only releasing me when they wanted to use me for their pleasure. Most days I was caned or spanked and sometimes I was whipped with a narrow leather strap. Every day I had to suck all of them. Finally, they threw me off the boat at Naples: ragged, destitute and dejected. As I walked the streets I was befriended by a young woman - a research student like me and about my age - who was working on a manuscript found recently in Pompeii. She let me stay with her and, as she worked translating the text from the original Latin and I recovered from my ordeal, I began recording her translation in the form of a story. The girl's supervisor, Dr Ahmad, a swarthy academic from Algeria was a cruel teacher. I used to watch through the heavy curtains, which were always drawn for their meetings, as she stood before him and read out her day's work. He scowled and never seemed pleased and often she ended up bent over his lap with her panties pulled down in a tangle around her ankles as he punished her for her shortcomings. I kept out of his way but, even so, perhaps when I prepared a meal and it was not quite to his taste or he did not like the colour of something I was wearing, I too felt the sting of his hand on my bare, upturned buttocks. I spent three months there and the product of this time is the story of *The Roman Slavegirl*.

Syra Bond. Naples. 2005

Chapter 1
The House of Slaves

Slightly inland from the soft blue haze of the Bay of Naples, and beneath the brooding cone of the sleeping Vesuvius stood Pompeii. Occupied by the Emperor Sulla in 89 BC it quickly became a Roman resort, dedicated to the fulfilment of pleasures of the flesh and inhabited by discerning patrons of the arts of depravity. It was to here that Romans flocked to have their sexual cravings fulfilled. There was a market for every vice and Olconio Rufo was the best-known supplier. Everyone that came to his fine house - to the richly mosaicked room at the rear of the atrium which he kept for meeting his clients - could be sure that whatever they requested would, if they were prepared to pay, be supplied.

Behind Rufo's house, along the high walled Street of Wolves that led to the Temple of Jupiter, were his slaves' quarters. The House of Slaves was a dark, windowless building crammed with women he had purchased either to sell on - perhaps to Africa or the town's brothels - or, if he thought they showed particular promise, to train for the specific requests of his most perverted and depraved customers. These women, from all corners of the Empire, worked on menial tasks until Rufo decided their fate.

Caristia was one of these unfortunates. Captured in Northern France early in 79AD and already a slave since childhood, she had been brought to Southern Italy because of her fine pale skin and her youth. And, as the trader that sold her to Rufo was keen to point out as she stood naked, humiliated and bound in chains in the market place, because she 'lifted her bottom for a spanking whenever she saw a hand'.

She had now been at Rufo's House of Slaves for several weeks.

'Pick that up slave!' shouted Magnus with relish as he brought the cane up behind his head. 'Pick it up!'

He paced towards Caristia across the dimly lit cellar where about twelve young, half naked women were straining to stack food and wine on high racks. The cane came down and caught the young girl - blue-eyed, flaxen-haired and slender - a glancing blow on her barely covered buttocks as she bent to pick up the bowl. She cowered as she reached out, hoping to avoid another blow, but from the resigned look on her face it was obvious she knew it was useless. Her bright blue eyes widened and her golden hair caught a glitter of sunlight as, her taut slender body frozen in fear and expectation, she awaited her fate. Ever since she had arrived in Pompeii - brought in through the Sea Gate, linked by chains in a trudging line of other slaves - and been sold to Rufo, she had been victimised by his vengeful slave master, Magnus Maximus. He stood above her, a towering African, himself brought from Nubia and sold into slavery but now, after years of faithful service, given his freedom by his rich and greedy master, Rufo.

'You are too slow,' he said, grinning broadly at the other slave women who all hung their heads silently, hoping they would not become his next target. He turned back to the flaxen-haired girl. 'It is true what they say. You invite the cane instead of avoiding it. You pretend to cower beneath me, but I can see in your eyes that you are wishing for more.'

'No master,' she said, grabbing the bowl and, staying on all fours, offering it to him compliantly in her right hand. 'I want only to do your bidding. That is my only wish, master, to serve you.'

He grinned again and lifted the cane. It glistened like a shaft of light in the yellow flickering gleam cast by the oil lamps placed in alcoves around the cellar. His black, freshly oiled body glittered; he looked like a god. His head was shaven smooth and his torso naked, his genitals barely covered by tight cotton cloth twisted at his waist and, beyond his heavily muscled legs, his feet were bound with the tight leather straps of his open sandals. He was an inspiring warrior, only spared combat in the arena when Rufo had discovered his talents for disciplining his female slaves. Magnus teased the end of the cane between his large white teeth then ran his tongue along its length. Caristia lowered the bowl and laid it on the floor as if realising the inescapability of punishment. Magnus smirked.

'Put down the bowl, little slave, and rest your hands on the floor.'

She did as she was told and, as she dipped her back, she raised her bottom slightly. He bent and lifted the tattered hem of her cotton smock, revealing her nakedness and her taut pale buttocks. He dropped the material into the small of her back then ran the tip of the cane against her bottom, tracing a white line across her smooth skin with its fine point. Aroused by its touch, as if by the promise of pain, she lifted her bottom higher, bending her elbows and dropping her shoulders until some of the spikes of her shock of blonde hair touched the cold stone floor.

'I am sorry master,' she whimpered, unable to disguise the racing of her heart in her fractured voice. 'I must be punished, I know it.'

He ran the tip of the cane around her buttocks, circling their pert beauty before again lifting the hem of the smock, pulling it up along her well-defined spine then dropping it down over her shoulders. As it fell, covering her head, she lowered her shoulders further and raised her buttocks higher. The dark crack between them opened and from the tantalising shadow the fleshy pink of her cunt was revealed - narrow and smooth and mounded up at the sides. Magnus ran the point of the cane along the delectable valley, prodding at her labia, testing their delicacy and, under the pressure of the cane they opened slightly and the slit at their centre glistened with her fragrant moisture. She sighed, a muffled sigh of compliance and let the side of her face rest submissively on the floor. She lay there, bent before him like a sacrifice.

Magnus lifted the cane above his head and paused. Caristia panted heavily, waiting for the cane to fall, knowing how much it would sting, how much it would burn and how much she would suffer until, finally, when he decided she had endured enough, it would end. She bit her lips and, warned by only the faintest swish of air, he brought it down fully across her naked bottom. She gasped as the stinging pain burned into her and she held her breath in an effort to stop herself from yelling too soon and as a way of bracing herself for the next. Her blue eyes widened when it fell, and she screwed up her face as the second lashing pain penetrated her but, as he raised the cane for the third time, she lifted her bottom still higher, opening the crack of her cunt and exposing her swelling flesh as much as she could for more.

He brought the cane down relentlessly but still she pushed her bottom up to meet it. No matter how hard it fell, how penetrating the pain, she still pushed herself at it, still lifted her buttocks, still exposed her cunt until she felt on fire, until she was burning with its heat. It scorched through her skin, up her neck and into her face. Then she sucked it in with gasping breaths and it entered her

4

very soul, filling her mind with images and driving her into a reverie of uncontrollable delight. She met each stroke with increasing ecstasy and when, finally, she sensed he would stop, she opened her buttocks wide, exposing the inner petals of her now soaking cunt and letting the stinging cane fall against its tender edges. His strokes built to a crescendo, lacing her tender flesh and, as if she had been unplugged, she felt the scream she had held in coursing up her throat. It broke free in a long penetrating screech and she collapsed, dropping fully to the floor, drenched by the flood of her own pent up, explosive orgasm, soaked by the bliss of pain.

As she panted and jerked under the shroud of her smock she felt Magnus running the tip of the cane along the red stripes that now covered her pale-skinned bottom. Her skin was so sensitised she squirmed at the slightest touch. She did not know whether he would start again, whether she had been punished enough, and she waited in case she must bear more - in case she must prepare herself for more ecstasy. But, as she heard him step back, she realised it was over and, still with her face covered, she sighed, rolled over and dropped her legs wide apart.

Magnus knelt down between them and turned to the other women.

'And now little ones, you can see her true reward. Here! You two! Come and hold her wrists. And you two! Hold her ankles.'

They ran forward obediently, but one took the lead. Bec, the captured daughter of the Dane Thorkell, tall and raven-haired, pushed the others aside so that she could take hold of Caristia first.

Caristia struggled as the women knelt and took hold of her. She felt their hands gripping her wrists and pulling her arms wide and she felt the exposure of her naked cunt as her ankles were held apart. She pulled herself from side to side in a desperate bid to remain free. Bec dug her nails into Caristia's ankles and glowered down at her menacingly; they had already fought over food and Bec had sworn to pay her back. Magnus rested forward on his hands and looked into Caristia's wide blue eyes. Caristia smelled his scent, myrrh and cloves, heady and strong and she felt his power. Not only his physical strength, which was immense, but his control of her, the subjugation of her will to his, and she gave a sudden gasp of apprehension as she realised her frailty.

He grabbed the tattered cloth of her smock that was still tangled up around her face and ripped it down the front. In one movement it was rent apart exposing her small firm breasts and flat stomach and, between her wide-spread legs and beneath the partial covering of delicate tousled pubic hair, the soft pink of her fleshy crack.

She pulled against the restraining hands of the other women but, even as she felt their unyielding tension, her desperation to escape ebbed as she felt the smouldering flames of excitement burning somewhere within her exposed body. She pulled again and this time - with the very act of tensioning her body - the flames of passion, of anticipation, licked around the swollen edges of her soft cunt, sensitising them like a caressing tongue, causing her to squirm not

5

only against the hands that held her but also against the heat that was flowing within her hips. Magnus dropped down and kissed her, licking her full lips with his own, driving his tongue into her mouth and searching out hers, analysing its response, testing her ability to hold back. He broke away, reared up like a massive cobra and drew a deep breath.

'See!' he shouted to the other women. 'You have no need to hold our little slave. Unless it is to hold her back! Yes! Her passion might even overcome the mighty Magnus. Keep a firm grip on her or she will jump up, wrestle me to the floor and overcome me!'

He grinned, then dropped and kissed her again. She felt the oiled skin of his muscular chest against her, rubbing against her nipples and hardening them. She felt his massive thighs against the inside of her own, wiping their oil against her, moistening her and, as he pressed himself closer, she felt the bulge of his cock. Already pounding inside his tight loincloth it pressed against the swollen edges of her cunt, pulling them apart, opening her up and making her ready. Still with his mouth firmly against hers and his tongue delving deeply inside, she felt his hand working its way to the base of her flat stomach. She felt his knuckles against her pubic hairs, pulling at them as they caught up between his fingers. Then she felt the heat of his cock as he lifted it from beneath his cotton loincloth and held it between the tops of her thighs. When he turned his hand over she felt his fingers prising apart the edges of her flesh and she felt them squeezing hard against the base of her throbbing, hardening clitoris. She squirmed beneath him, struggling against the women as they held her fast, fighting them but now not wanting to escape. Now she wanted to release herself so that she was free to reach up and encircle him with her arms. To wrap her legs around his hips, to draw herself up onto him and drive herself onto his stiff, pulsating cock until she was so full it would be impossible to cram any more inside her. She struggled again and the tension of restraint only increased her desire. She pushed her hips at him, searching out the mass of his cock, wriggling herself around its end, working to insert it into herself. She struggled to enclose its heat, but it was hopeless, she was held too tightly. She moaned under his bulk, holding her breath as he continued to kiss her, hoping he would force his cock into her quickly and deliver her from the punishment of frustration.

He reached beneath her and lifted her buttocks. She felt stretched against her captors, as if straining on a crucifix. He wedged one hand beneath her waist, keeping her clear of the floor. Then, as he drove his cock into her - setting her on fire, filling her with burning delight - he smacked her bottom rhythmically, mirroring each push of his cock in her cunt with a heavy, resounding smack across her squirming buttocks. Each slap, each stinging strike of his huge flat hand, drove her further into delirium. Every time it landed she tightened more, tensing with the shock, stunned by the pain. But, even as she was filled with the anguish of hurt, she was suffused with the delights of the ecstasy of pleasure. Each stinging blow, each shrieking withdrawal from the source, each muscular spasm only mixed with the delightful throbbing in her cunt and transported her further into a heaven of shrieking bliss. She sucked at his tongue, dragging it to the back of her throat and she rode up as much as she could onto his cock, now filling and pulsating with the surging tide of his oncoming orgasm. She tightened her hips, hanging onto his pounding cock, keeping it deep inside her, drawing at it, making herself ready to drain the flow of semen that would soon drench the inside of her hot wet cunt. She pictured it filling her and, when at last she felt its heat spurting from his pulsating cock, she rose up onto it for a last time. She squeezed herself onto his cock and, with a dragging exhalation and a massive visceral shudder, she released her own convulsive orgasm. She hung there as he finished, jerking and shaking, allowing him to fill her, allowing him to set her on fire and, only when he pulled out and she felt the dribble of semen running stickily on the insides of her legs, did she relax slightly and allow her buttocks to fall back onto the cold stone floor.

'You have found me another one then, my dear Magnus,' shouted a finely dressed man as he entered the cellar. All the women except Bec dropped away in deference, bowing their heads and backing against the rough stone walls. They looked frightened and pitiful; some with their breasts exposed, others with barely a rag pulled around their waists and several completely naked. 'Let me see her,' the man ordered, standing above Magnus. 'You have not allowed me a full view yet.' He stood above Bec as she opened her mouth and showed her teeth to Caristia. 'Magnus! Move this one. Is she out of control? Surely you have not lost your touch. I think she needs some discipline.'

'Yes master. No master Rufo.' stuttered Magnus, getting to his feet and bowing his head.

'Magnus, there is no need to call me master. You are a free man. No matter. I expect you to keep my little savages under control. Remind me of your talents. Let me see you bring this one who bares her teeth to heel.'

Magnus grabbed Bec by the arm and tried to force her onto her knees. She resisted and, as she was twisted sideways she sank her teeth into his forearm. He looked more astonished than in pain as he watched the blood flowing down onto the back of his hand then, suddenly, his expression changed and a fire of redness lit up in his dark eyes as he realised that this was a challenge to his authority.

'On your knees!' he shouted.

'Magnus!' taunted Rufo. 'Beware! She has the teeth of a wolf and is ready to pounce at you again.'

Caristia edged away, pulling herself backwards with her stinging bottom against the cold floor. She glanced at Bec who, as soon as she caught her eye, lurched at Caristia, desperate to break free from Magnus so she could attack her real enemy - not the controlling Magnus but her rival, Caristia.

'What is wrong with the woman, Magnus?' shouted Rufo gleefully. 'She is more like a gladiator than a servant. Perhaps we should be training her for the ring instead of the bed chamber.'

'I will discipline her, master. She will not get the better of me I assure you.'

'Then discipline her. Let me see her brought to heel. Let me see her keeping her bare white teeth behind those full and luscious lips. Let me see her prepared to service the needs of a man and not the needs of her own wolf-like appetite.' He held his hand beneath her chin, squeezing her cheeks slightly and glaring into her wild eyes, then as he saw her making ready to spit, he released her and turned away. 'Discipline her!'

Magnus grabbed Bec by the arm and twisted her round. She fought him but he was so powerful that, in one movement, he wrapped both her wrists behind her back and held them there in one of his huge hands.

'Now slave,' he said looking into her eyes, 'I will show my master how you can be subdued.'

Still holding her hands behind her back with one hand, and with his elbow pressing between her shoulder blades, he bent her down over his crooked knee. Her breasts, for all their tautness, dropped forward with the shock of the forward thrust and Caristia stared at Bec's proud nipples, reddened by her frustration and throbbing with her passion to fight. Bec kicked her legs frantically but, as she bared her teeth and spat at the staring Caristia, Magnus brought his right leg together with his left and secured her, as if in a vice, between his muscular thighs. He brought his free hand down on her tense bottom with a loud smack. She tensed, tightening herself against the trap that held her, but she did not alter the expression on her face, all the time staring hard at Caristia as if trying to burn her with her gaze.

Magnus spanked her hard, each time bringing his hand down more firmly. The loud smacks caused Bec to tense until she was rigid, but she did not cry out, nor did she squirm or try to avoid the blows. Caristia looked at Bec's taut body and listened to the regular rhythm of Magnus's smacking hand. She leant back against the wall, almost hidden by the shadows, and allowed her fingers to drift between her legs. She felt the soft insides of her thighs then, slowly working them upwards, she met the crack of her cunt. It was wet and still dripping with semen, but now a fresh moisture was glistening on her swollen pink flesh. As she exposed herself in the half light of the lamps her cunt glistened with the dampness of excitement brought on by the sight of Bec: rigid, clasped between Magnus's massive thighs, staring fixedly ahead at her adversary, bearing the pain and showing how she could stand it and any amount more.

Caristia worked her fingers into the soft folds of her outer labia, teasing them apart, finding the silky wetness on their inside edges and seeking out her clitoris - uncovered already - exposed to the glancing touch of her fingertips, growing with expectation, making her pant. She dropped her legs wider and saw Bec staring between them. She wanted her trapped enemy to look at her cunt as she opened it, revealing its inner leaves, showing the darkness of her throbbing clitoris, letting Bec delve into it with her eyes. Each smack that landed on Bec's buttocks, each extra tensing it brought about in her unyielding body, led

Caristia to delve her fingers further. Her eyes widened as she squirmed onto the full stretch of her fingers, all the time staring at the object of her desire; the prone, dribbling Bec. She pulled her fingers up and down, caressing the inside of her vagina then, as she sensed the beating coming to an end, she held them stiffly, thrust them up to the knuckles and dropped herself onto them, finishing in a silent, heavy, throbbing orgasm.

Magnus released Bec, dropping her to the floor, her buttocks reddened and angry. He reached down as she fell and he pinched her nipples between his thumbs and fingers, but still she stared unswervingly at Caristia.

'She needs the cane, master; she will not be subdued by a simple hand,' said Magnus.

'Then you must leave her punishment until later. For the moment I wish to see this little one who is, by the looks of it, already excited by what she sees. Or has her passion been released by my presence, Magnus?'

Caristia pulled her hands from between her legs as Rufo turned towards her.

'Yes master,' said Magnus, stepping over Bec and growling at her in annoyance. 'It is surely your presence.'

'Magnus, I remind you again that you are a free man now,' said Rufo with some irritation. 'You do not need to call me master. You should call me Olconio Rufo. Say it now: "Olconio Rufo".'

'Yes,' Magnus hesitated, embarrassed. 'Yes, Olconio Rufo,' he stuttered slowly and with much discomfort.

'Now, stand aside, clear this indolent one out of the way and tell me about this pretty little maid you have selected - and already tried out for me. Who is she, Magnus?'

Magnus kicked out and Bec reluctantly dropped back, still glowering at Caristia but no longer baring her teeth and no longer struggling to attack her. She put her hands against her bottom but not to rub them, to assuage the pain, but to show that she was untroubled by the beating, that she held it in contempt. Magnus was angered by her scorn but had to ignore her.

'Master,' Magnus faltered as Rufo smiled at him tolerantly. 'She is one of the youngest here and from Northern France. You purchased her three weeks ago from the market. '

'Yes? Yes?'

'She likes the feel of a man's hand across her buttocks, sir. She likes the cane as well, but especially she likes a hand.'

'How does she feel? Is she well fleshed? Is she moist?'

'Yes sir, she is, as moist as silk, and she rises onto a man's member like a tide, like a rushing sea eager to come into the shore.'

Rufo laughed at Magnus's poetry.

'You are a romantic, Magnus. You should take up philosophy. Now, could she be trained?'

'Yes sir, without doubt.'

'Sit up girl,' ordered Rufo. 'Let me see you properly. Tell me your name.'

Caristia got up onto her knees and bowed her head. Her torn smock was still bundled up around her waist and she saw Magnus's glistening semen, mixed with her own moisture, still running stickily down the insides of her thighs. She still felt his heat inside her cunt and she took a deep breath in an effort to calm herself.

'Caristia, master.'

'You are indeed a pretty one. I wonder if you are as interesting as Magnus says.'

He turned her slowly by the shoulders. She clasped her hands together submissively and laid them gently against her pubic hair, covering her wet cunt as she folded her fingers between her legs and into its crack. Her eyes rolled slightly as she felt the warmth of her fingertips slipping inside the silky folds of her flesh and, even as he continued to turn her, she let her fingers delve a little deeper.

Rufo looked into her bright blue eyes.

'She is very young, Magnus. How has she picked up the skills you say she has?'

'It is the breed, sir. The northern tribes are born to it.'

Rufo pushed her shoulders forward, bending her at the waist so he could see her bottom fully. She did not resist, but dropped forward, keeping her hands where they were and allowing her head to almost touch her knees. Rufo smoothed his hand across her taut bottom and she opened her buttocks at his touch, revealing her delving fingers between the flesh of her moist crack. He rubbed her buttocks more and she responded with a sigh, an expectant moan drawn only from desire, and she drove her fingers deeper.

'You are right my friend,' said Rufo, pleased. 'She is indeed special.' He pressed his fingertip against her anus and it opened for him, dilating in a neat dark circle as she lifted higher as an offering. She wanted his finger inside, penetrating her as deeply as it would go, and she sighed again as she thought of being filled. She bent as far forward as she could, showing him the moist crack of her cunt, glistening and pink and opened by her own fingers and exposing her anus, a dark recess of delight. He pressed his finger in and she rode up on it, moaning loudly as he pushed, in one thrust, up to the knuckle. She squirmed on his hand, feeling her clitoris with wet frantic fingers, moaning, dribbling, needing more. He brought his other hand down on her tight bottom in a loud smack and the shock and sharpness made her squeeze her buttocks together, clamping his finger deeply inside her anus and causing shivers of bliss to penetrate deeply into her shaking body. Another loud smack and she squeezed onto his finger even tighter. Then another and she shouted out, not in pain but in eagerness, hanging onto his finger in her anus, feeling it so deep, feeling so full, but still wanting more. She craved to finish yet was desperate to hold herself in that enchanting moment of anticipation, inhabiting that heavenly state of delicious frustration.

Magnus stood in front of her and she smelled his body as he lifted his hard cock towards her mouth. She let him force it right to the back of her throat before closing her mouth around it. When she did encircle it with her lips she felt its pulsating veins sending shockwaves around her face. Rufo kept up the beating, smacking her as hard as he could, each time knocking her forward onto Magnus's cock. She gulped between each heavy smack then, as she felt her face reddening with the fire of her own orgasm, Magnus's throbbing cock expanded in her mouth and filled her with a flood of semen. Even though there was barely enough room for it to squeeze past the massive cock that forced her mouth as wide as it would go, it ran from the sides of her mouth. It dribbled and ran onto her chin and, as the pace of the smacking increased, she rose up on Rufo's stiff finger for a last time and submitted to the joy of a jerking, convulsive orgasm.

Rufo took his finger out of Caristia's anus and she hung before him, bent and dissipated, gasping for breath with semen running from her trembling mouth. Rufo moved back and smiled.

'Magnus, she is indeed special. From now on keep little Caristia at her tasks but set aside a time each day for special training. I will supervise it myself. I am meeting some clients this afternoon and have some interesting ideas to put to them. And Magnus, make sure that she feels the flat of your hand every day; we do not want her to lose her keenness from lack of use. No, do not let her go without. She may have to miss her food but do not hold back on her spanking.' Magnus bowed his head, unable to do otherwise, and Rufo, smiling at his old slave's continued unconquerable subservience, turned to go. 'Oh, and the other one, the one who got the better of you, our little spitting wolf. Such spirit, so unlike the delectable little Caristia and yet so complementary. Make sure she is caned and then bring her to me. Like her little opponent, her future is already decided.'

Chapter 2

Caristia is taken into training

All Rufo's guests reclined on the elegant couches, propping themselves up on their left elbows as custom demanded, all looking eager for their evening meal, the only main meal of the day. They had spent the afternoon in the main Stabian Baths, luxuriating themselves in the steam rooms, having their skin scraped clean by young male slaves, plunging headlong into freezing pools of crystal clear water and finally, being massaged by the powerful hands of Turkish eunuchs whose lives were dedicated to their art. Now, facing in towards the low tables decked with fastidiously prepared food, they were all ravenous.

'Rufo, I hear you have some fresh stock,' said a young man, barely out of his twenties with rich black hair and, as was conventional, a short growth of dark beard. 'And some interesting ones at that, apparently.' He laughed as he took a glass of wine mixed with water from a dark-haired young slavegirl. He held her thin wrist as she reached forward to serve him, and she pulled back instinctively against his firm grip. 'More willing than this one, I think,' he said, laughing as he let her go and she rushed away red-faced and embarrassed to refill the serving amphora.

'Dear Lucretius Fronto, how do you get to hear of these things? You must have spies all over Pompeii,' said Rufo, beckoning the flustered and frightened Innocenti to refill his glass. 'Sometimes I think some of my own slaves must be in your pay.' The young girl hurried over and tipped the blue glass amphora until the lemon-coloured wine gurgled freely over the carefully shaped neck. 'Careful girl!' shouted Rufo as some of the wine spilled onto his hand. 'Careful!'

'If this is one of your new girls, my dear Olconio Rufo, the only interesting thing she demonstrates is her stupidity.' Rufo's face tightened in anger. 'Perhaps the talents of your new slave is disobedience Rufo,' mocked Fronto.

'Kneel girl!' Rufo shouted at Innocenti. 'At my feet.' The young girl knelt nervously and hung her head, exposing her small breasts in the fold of her loose, open-necked tunic. She licked her lips edgily and her hands shook with fear.

'Such obedience, my dear Rufo. No wonder your services are sought throughout Pompeii,' jeered the young man. 'If this is the quality of your stock, my friend, I do not think you will be parting me from any of my money.'

Rufo scowled at Innocenti and she flushed as she felt the heat of his stare.

'Bend over, girl!' he shouted angrily. 'You will be punished for your disobedience!' Innocenti flinched at the loudness of his voice, then keeping her knees together, she dropped forward obediently onto her still shaking hands. The low neck of her tunic opened more, revealing the small points of her hardened nipples as they tightened with her increasing anxiety. 'Magnus!' shouted Rufo. 'Bring in Caristia to serve while I punish this one.'

Magnus entered the room with Caristia on a short lead tied to a collar around her slender neck. She looked around fleetingly then dropped her bright blue eyes and followed Magnus as he led her to a serving table. She wore a short white tunic and looked fragile and delicate as she walked obediently behind him. Fronto obviously noticed her, and was clearly taken by her Saxon charm, but he was keen to taunt Rufo more and pretended to ignore her.

'Ah, Magnus,' said Fronto, picking up a fig and carefully teasing it apart to reveal the pink inner flesh. 'A free man now, I believe. Rufo, you are indeed an emancipated soul. There are no slaves in my household who will ever gain their freedom I can assure you. Not a one. Consider yourself fortunate, Magnus, that you had a soft master.'

'Well, my splendid guest,' said Rufo, both annoyed and embarrassed by Fronto's continued criticism. 'Tell me your desires and I will be surprised if they are not readily available from my little harem.'

'From what I have seen I will be surprised if they are, my friend. Even so, for my own amusement I will tell you.'

Caristia stood where she had been left by Magnus, the leather leash trailing from the collar at her neck and her eyes taking fleeting and secretive glances around the room. She had never seen such richness before and she shook with excitement as the finely dressed, reclining men picked at the food laid out on the low tables. Fronto looked at her and, although she dropped her eyes quickly she was unable to prevent a faint red flush of embarrassment covering her face and chest. He smiled but still ignored her.

'Proceed then,' urged Rufo, sipping his wine. 'We are all waiting for the benefit of your wisdom on these matters.'

'First, my friend, I would like to see the wretch at your feet punished.'

Rufo bent and lifted the hem of Innocenti's tunic. Her bottom was smooth and taut and the tight crack between her buttocks was an appetising valley that, with her knees close together, revealed nothing of her other delights. Only the slightest gap was apparent at the top of her thighs and that, so small - so delicate a triangle of space - that not even a wisp of her pubic hair could be seen in its sheltering sanctuary. Rufo smoothed his hand across both her cheeks, feeling their firmness, testing their elasticity as he would the skin on a drum. He smiled to himself, as if the touch of young flesh reminded him of everything that was good in his life and he breathed in deeply, as if inhaling her very essence.

'Do you realise you have done wrong?' he asked Innocenti.

'Yes, master,' she replied nervously. 'I am sorry.'

'But sadly that is not enough. You see my fine guest wants to see you suffer for your misdeeds and I cannot disappoint him.'

Innocenti screwed up her eyes as if she was already feeling the stinging pain of his hand across her bottom.

Rufo pulled the hem of her tunic higher, exposing her narrow hips and slim waist before dropping it back between her shallow shoulder blades. Caristia lifted her head slightly and looked at Innocenti. Her frailty, her submission and her impending punishment conspired to excite Caristia and, as she saw the pink, hard tips of the young girl's nipples glancing against the thin material of her loose tunic she felt a growing moistness between the satiny edges of her cunt. She lifted her head higher and leant forward against the leather collar that was bound tightly around her neck. The constriction caused her to catch her breath but she did not ease back.

Rufo smiled at Fronto, then without further warning brought his hand down across the girl's bottom. It smacked loudly against her youthful skin and instantly she dipped her back, tightening her buttocks and squirming with pain.

'Stay still!' Rufo shouted angrily as Fronto laughed at the girl's weakness. 'Your master has ordered you. Stay still!'

Innocenti lifted her bottom as much as she could, but she was already shaking all over and could not keep properly still. She bit her lips and screwed up her eyes even tighter but this time tears squeezed from her eyelids and ran down her cheeks as she began to whimper.

'I see the girl is the pick of your crop, my friend,' jeered Fronto with delight. 'Perhaps you would like me to discipline her for you. That is if she is too much for you!'

Rufo's outrage increased and, when he brought his hand down again, his eyes were bulging and his face was red with anger. His heavy palm met Innocenti's buttocks - blotched red from the first blow - with an even louder smack and she fell forward, wriggling to avoid another and struggling to stem the burning pain that now enveloped her. She stretched out her arms and pulled up her knees in a frantic effort to get away. Caristia looked between Innocenti's sprawling legs and saw, at the top of her now outspread thighs, the fine neat crack of her cunt and the hint of the light pinkness at its centre. The sight of it sent a thrill through Caristia's hips and she squirmed, without thinking, and pressed both hands between her legs and against her own wet cunt.

'She is a weak one indeed,' taunted Fronto. 'But even so, she has the strength to escape you. She will wriggle away like an eel, my friend, unless you catch her and make her secure.'

Fronto made a grab for Innocenti and caught hold of her ankle but she clawed at the floor, grabbing the leg of a low table and straining to get away. As all the guests roared with laughter Fronto's patience snapped.

'Magnus! Magnus! Take hold of this wretch. Bend her over your back so I can give her the thrashing she deserves.'

Magnus grabbed the writhing Innocenti as she kicked at Rufo to try and shake him off. He picked her up like a leaf, bent her slightly forward and in one deft movement pulled her over his back, holding each of her arms down tightly over his shoulders so that her body hung, face-forward and secure.

'Well horsed!' shouted Fronto enthusiastically. 'Now we shall see who the master is! Rufo or the little eel!' Rufo, still flustered, grabbed a tightly bound bunch of sticks that hung near the entrance. 'You choose the *fasces*, Rufo!' exclaimed Fronto excitedly. 'Good! Good!'

Innocenti looked back to see what was happening. Her face was filled with fear and tears streamed down her pale cheeks. Caristia felt a penetrating wave of excitement spread through her as she witnessed the young girl's plight. It travelled from her hips into her chest, tightening her already hardened nipples and squeezing her throat as if it were a hand. She inserted two fingers into her wet cunt and dropped herself onto them forcibly.

'Hold her tight Magnus!' shouted Rufo as he raised the bundle of sticks behind his head. 'Tight!'

Magnus pulled Innocenti's arms down hard against his massive chest and, as she gasped for breath and threw her head from side to side, Rufo brought the *fasces* down across her stretched buttocks. She screamed and strained back against Magnus's unbreakable grip as a heavy red blotch with spiky edges appeared on her left buttock. Caristia felt moisture running on the soft edges of her swollen cunt and let her jaw drop as she pressed her fingers deeper.

Magnus pulled harder on Innocenti's arms and Rufo brought the *fasces* down again. It landed with a heavy smack and Innocenti gasped and twisted in a frenzy as her right buttock was reddened like the other. Again Rufo brought the bundle of canes down, deepening the redness and accentuating the lines that spread out onto Innocenti's hips. Again he brought it down, and again, each time seeking out fresh pale flesh and reddening the tops of her thighs and her back as if she had been scorched. Each blow was harder and each time Innocenti threw herself into a violent, writhing fit, but her cries for mercy were hopeless, there was no escape and the punishment was relentless. She screamed as she was filled with nothing but pain and gradually, as the blows continued, she weakened and hung loosely on Magnus's back.

Caristia could not keep her eyes from the red-smeared body of the suffering girl. Each blow thrilled her, each resounding smack of the bundle of canes made her drive her fingers deeper, and each screech, or shrieking gasp of breath heightened her excitement and brought her closer to the delight of a desperately craved final ecstasy. She looked at Fronto as he leant forward and clapped his hands with approval, and she stared between his bare legs at the shape of his fleshy genitals outlined beneath his short tunic.

Finally Rufo stopped and Innocenti hung, barely conscious, against Magnus's back. She twitched but no longer squirmed to escape.

'I think she has had her lesson,' announced Rufo, throwing the *fasces* to the floor and lifting a glass of wine to his dry mouth.

'Hardly!' sneered Fronto. 'I thought you had only just started!' He waved towards Caristia. 'Here slave.' Caristia, knowing he saw what she was doing, swallowed hard and pulled her fingers from her aching cunt. She was unsure what to do and looked wide-eyed at Rufo for instructions. He nodded his assent and she walked towards Fronto. 'Now this is a pretty one I grant you, Rufo.' He grabbed her breasts and squeezed her hard nipples. 'And she has been pleasuring herself, I think.' He squeezed her nipples again and she gasped with the thrill of his harsh touch. 'Now girl, stand here.'

He ordered Magnus to drop Innocenti and she slid from his back like an unwanted load. She crouched on her knees and looked beseechingly with tear-filled eyes at her master, but he ignored her. There was a moment of silence, as if the wretched girl would be saved, but suddenly she twisted around sharply as Fronto grabbed her by the hair and dragged her over to Caristia. He lifted Caristia's tunic up over her head and dropped it to the floor. She felt a wave of delight run through her body as her nakedness was exposed to everyone and she moved her legs slightly apart to ease the growing heat in her cunt. Fronto ripped Innocenti's tunic down and kicked it aside dismissively. She was still shaking with the pain of the thrashing and her mouth was trembling. She pushed her hands between her legs in a pathetic attempt to cover herself, but she was shaking so much she could not keep them in place. Fronto made Caristia and Innocenti stand back to back. He linked their arms together at the elbows then, with the assistance of one of the other guests, pulled their wrists together in front of their stomachs and bound them tightly with thin leather cords. Caristia felt the heat of Innocenti's sobbing body tight against her back and bottom and shivered with excitement and expectancy.

'Now,' said Fronto, turning to the other guests. 'I will show you what a real thrashing is.' He stood in front of Caristia and smiled. He reached forward and pinched her nipples, and as he pressed his thumbs and fingers harder he saw the gasping, open-eyed look of pained delight on her face. He dropped to his knees, forced her thighs wide and pressed his mouth tightly against her cunt. He licked it deeply, penetrating the soft folds of her outer labia easily and delving between the silky inner petals before finding the soft, dark recesses within. She lifted herself up from his mouth, but not to escape his lips and tongue. She lifted herself to lessen the contact of her flesh against them in an attempt to control the ecstasy that their caress brought on. But as she squirmed her hips to rise up - to make the contact of her fleshy cunt with his tongue a little fainter - the movement of her hips and the pressure of her buttocks around her dilating anus only accentuated her bliss and she felt herself burning with the rush of an oncoming orgasm. She tried again to move away but the her swollen labia stuck softly to his lips and tugged gently at the satin-like inner folds of her cunt and she froze, unable to do anything but wait for the flooding pleasure within to burst.

Fronto drew back and looked up at her. 'I look up to you as if you were my mistress. Madam,' he mocked, 'does my mistress like my tongue inside her? Perhaps you could do me the honour of bending forward and lifting the little slave on to your back so I can thrash her for her weakness.' Caristia felt the muscles at the sides of her stomach contracting and she bit her lips to try and suppress the waves of pleasure that were sweeping threw her. 'Madam,' he repeated. 'Madam, you keep me waiting. Perhaps the answer is in your cunt.' He slurped noisily at her and she rose in a sudden convulsion of pleasure. The guests laughed and Fronto jumped to his feet athletically. 'Bend over, slave,' he said, changing his tone. 'Lift the little one up onto your back. Do as I ordered!'

Caristia hesitated for a moment, still shivering with the rapture of her pleasure, and Fronto took her nipples between his thumbs and fingers, pinched them hard and pulled her forward, bending her at the hip as the slight form of Innocenti was lifted up onto Caristia's back and off the floor.

Innocenti bent backwards as she was lifted, stretching her small frame in an outward curve from her head to her feet. Her breasts flattened against her chest and her flat stomach shallowed between her hips. The mound above the slit of her pink cunt, naked except for the merest wisps of soft pubic hair, was accentuated as her slight body strained against the opposing curve of Caristia's bent back. As Caristia bent further Innocenti opened her legs to prevent herself falling off and the soft pink of her cunt was fully exposed between the tops of her pale thighs. Fronto rubbed his hand down her body, first stroking her narrow neck then pawing across her chest and her stomach before stopping at the mound of her cunt. He tugged at the insubstantial pubic hair and she winced as much in shock as in pain. He pulled it again, harder, and she screwed up her

16

teary eyes in hopeless despair. He laid his hand fully across her cunt, squeezing its soft edges between his fingers before pinching the flesh sharply between the nails of his thumb and forefinger. Innocenti cried out, an expression of violation, but it was a faint cry - a cry of resignation as much as it was a cry of pain.

Fronto reached down and grabbed her ankles. He pulled her legs together and lifting them high until Innocenti's supine form was bent up at right angles, her taut buttocks rested above Caristia's as Caristia remained bent forward, holding the weight of the terrified girl on her back. Fronto ran his fingers down Innocenti's legs, from her ankles, between her taut calves and thighs then running them into the slit of her cunt, between the cheeks of her bottom then finally down between Caristia's buttocks. He lifted Innocenti's ankles higher, stretching her upwards, tightening the flesh of her cunt and stretching the pale skin of her bottom tight. He rubbed his hand against her cunt again, then drew his hand back and slapped her hard. She tightened the cheeks of her bottom even closer together and let out a whinnying cry of shock. Again he smacked her, harder this time, and Innocenti reared up, curling slightly on Caristia's back as she was filled with the stinging pain of her tormentor's hand. Again he smacked her, loud and heavy and her buttocks reddened as another one fell, and another. He kept her ankles high, tensioning her bottom, making it tight and firm and ensuring that each blow fell precisely where he intended and each smack delivered the maximum amount of pain.

Innocenti writhed as the smacking blows continued to fall against her buttocks and Caristia opened her legs to make sure she did not stumble under the squirming weight of the tender young girl on her back. It was as though it was never going to stop, as if Fronto would beat her all night, but in the end, as her cries became fainter and the tension in her body slackened, he stopped. He kept holding her ankles high, looking at her reddened buttocks with satisfaction, then he opened her legs wide. Her pink cunt was exposed fully, cradled in the redness of her burning bottom, its edges now swollen and with the faint darkness of pubic hair barely visible. He prised the flesh open with his fingers and teased the base of her clitoris. She shouted out again, as if his touch was a prelude to further pain, but her cry turned quickly to a whimper and then a moan. He laughed, lifted his white toga and offered his veiny cock to the wet opening.

Caristia felt the heat of his balls as they hung down against the top of her buttocks, then as he opened Innocenti's labia wide and inserted the tip of his throbbing glans, she felt them pressing against her skin and the heat and pressure made her gulp with anticipation. She tried to widen her buttocks, to open herself up to him, to allow his heavy balls to rub against the soft inner edges, perhaps glance against her dilated anus, but as he drove his cock into the girl's cunt Caristia had to grab her knees tightly to stop herself falling.

Fronto pushed his cock in hard and Innocenti screamed; it was her first time, nothing had entered her before and the suddenness and depth of penetration were unknown, shocking and overwhelming. She felt as if she had been rent apart and she choked as though filled to her mouth. He kept up the pressure, driving his cock up and down her wet cunt, opening it, using its freshness, destroying her virginity. He braced her legs back against her chest with his forearm and, bending her knees against her breasts, he started spanking her again. Each thrust brought another smack, another scorching spank against her upturned bottom, and with each one he lifted her higher on his cock as her satiny flesh, and her pitiful cries, brought him closer to fulfilment.

Innocenti yelled loudly, unable to distinguish pain from pleasure, lost in a maelstrom of sensations, spinning in a dizzy world of unknown pleasures then, as if snatched up by a sudden storm, she reared back, lifted her hips and shook with her first ever convulsing orgasm. It ran through her in waves as Fronto continued to thrust his cock deeper and she pulled hard against Caristia's elbows as if the pressure against her arms was all that would keep her alive. She felt the massive cock throbbing inside waiting to deliver the product of Fronto's pleasure, waiting to saturate her with semen, but she did not know what to expect, what to prepare for. She felt it expanding at the end, thickening along the veiny shaft and stuffing her so full she thought it would never come, but she did not know what to expect, what form the deluge of his orgasm would take. She shouted out, unrecognisable words from her own unknown language as again the fresh sensation of her second orgasm snatched her up, as if borne on a tempest, then threw her down onto the cock that was now swelling with the pulsating of flowing semen.

Fronto pressed down on her, bending her legs until her shins touched her tearstained cheeks then, spanking her all the time, harder and harder, he suddenly strained back, tightened every muscle in his body and pushed his cock as deep as it would go. Innocenti's eyes widened like globes and, as again her face reddened and the pale skin of her chest flushed with another deluge of ecstasy, she felt the burst of soaking heat inside her cunt as he drenched her with a massive flow of hot, sticky semen.

Caristia gasped as she felt the pressure against her back, then as Fronto pulled his cock out of Innocenti's cunt, Caristia felt the dripping gush of semen running into the crack of her buttocks. It poured between them then, still hot, it flowed against the rear of her swollen flesh. She opened her legs a little, encouraging it to run between her labia and, as she dipped her hips to open herself more, she felt it running around the base of her hard and throbbing clitoris.

Suddenly Caristia felt herself being manhandled and, still interlocked back to back with Innocenti, she was laid down on her side. Ropes were fetched and the two females were bound together at the waist then rolled over so that Caristia was on top and Innocenti was beneath, face forward and pressed against the floor. Caristia screeched as her legs were lifted and she felt the full force of the *fasces* come down on her buttocks, and she screeched again as a second blow followed immediately. Fronto and one of his guests were beating her together.

She writhed against the blows as they fell one after another on either side of her buttocks but, as the pain increased - as the punishing flames licked against the edges of her cunt - she lifted her bottom higher and opened herself for more. Others joined in and more bunches of sharp sticks flogged the backs of her thighs and her breasts. The stinging contact filled her body with heat, burning every part of her until, brought on by both the exposure and degradation as well as the burning and humiliating pain, she felt the beginning of her first long orgasm. She screamed as it gripped her and she jerked with the ecstasy of it, as much fulfilled by the knowledge that it was only a prelude as the remorseless beating continued.

Fronto knelt between her legs and drove his throbbing cock into her cunt first, but even as he was finishing and semen was running against the inside of her legs another guest took his place. Each one that came inside her made her finish and each orgasm, each burst of bliss, drove her to want more. She wrapped her legs around each one, holding him as deep and for as long as possible and she held her buttocks up as much as she could to feel the burning heat of the thrashing *fasces* on her red-striped skin.

Finally, when they had all used her, and she was reddened by the beating and covered with semen, she was released from Innocenti. Innocenti was tied between two marble pillars, gagged so that she could not scream and thrashed with a cane until she fell unconscious. Magnus was ordered to hold Caristia upside down. Clasping her around the waist and, holding her face outwards at knee height, he carried her from guest to guest. Each one pushed his cock into her mouth and finished either in her mouth or on her face. When she had been taken to them all semen ran from her lips and dripped onto the floor. In the end, when Magnus was ordered to release her, he cradled her gently and she felt, even amid the pleasure of her dissipation, the warmth of his kindness to her.

Fronto pinched Caristia's nipples as she licked the semen from her lips and swallowed it.

'I will buy this little Saxon, my dear Rufo. I do not think she is worth much but I am prepared to train her to be useful. Perhaps as a serving maid.'

'You are very kind, my dear Fronto,' said Rufo, determined that Fronto should not have her. 'But I am afraid she is not for sale. I have already promised her. Take the young Innocenti. Although she is weak you have seen how much she can suffer, and she will not cost much.'

'She is a sorry purchase, dear Rufo, but I do not want to be ungrateful. You have entertained us well and it would be unappreciative of me not to buy something from you. Yes, I will take her and, because of her weakness, you can be sure I will treat her kindly.' He smirked at the other guests. 'She will be offered daily to my dinner guests for a spanking and she will be forced to lick and suck all their cocks. If they are displeased she will be laid across the dinner table and caned then made to do it again until everyone is satisfied. After we are tired of her I will send her to service my gladiators, where I will have her suspended on ropes with her legs widespread so that she can be easily lowered onto their cocks. Every night, when she is returned to her quarters, I will have her spanked so hard she will yell louder than the beasts who are tortured and killed in the arena. Then, during the night, I will allow any of my male slaves to use her in any way they wish.'

'She is yours now, my friend. You must do with her as you will,' said Rufo, already going over in his mind the new plans he had for Caristia.

Innocenti had a rope pulled around her neck and she was led out by Fronto's manservant. She looked back emptily at Caristia. Her raised eyebrows and the sad look from her dark eyes was an appeal for help, but it was an appeal void of meaning, a plea in which was written only hopelessness.

Each day after Fronto's visit Caristia was taken to Rufo's house. Sometimes she was stripped naked and made to stand in front of erotic mosaics in a small private room where daily he met his customers. The pictures were made from the smallest of coloured tiles and depicted men with massive cocks, some tied up with leather straps with women sucking them, holding them and riding them as if possessed by a frenzy. It was as though these women had been possessed by the gods and were struggling to accomplish a god's passions while confined in a human body. It was as if they could not contain the heavenly fire within them, taking them over, forcing them to do more than they could, in the end, ever stand.

If Caristia moved while she was standing there Rufo's guests would beat her, spanking her over their knees or bending her over a chair and caning her. Often she was brought to dinner on all fours and kept like that all evening. Sometimes she had a small purse hung around her neck and Rufo's guests put their sexual requests into it then drew them out and discussed which ones to demand. Once she was held under the water in the pool in the atrium then spanked by all the guests before they tied her to a column and forced their cocks first into her cunt then into her mouth, one by one. Some of them sprayed their semen into a bowl and she was made to drink it. Once she was sent to crawl through the streets with a sign hanging from her neck saying that for the payment of one *sesterce* anyone who wished could spank her. Late that night, unable to find her way back, she was found by a group of young men who tied her to the wheel of a cart and beat her with canes. Magnus drove the men away and took her almost unconscious body back to the slaves' quarters in his arms.

One day, after she had been held down and beaten across the breasts and cunt, by some rich friends of Rufo's, Caristia saw Bec being taken from the house by Magnus. Her wrists were bound and she was tightly gagged with a leather strap, but it was not enough to stem her fury and she fought against Magnus like a wild beast. She braced herself against the doorway and kicked out at him, and he had to beat her with a *fasces* in order to get her outside. As Bec spit and snarled at Magnus, even when he was thrashing her as hard as he could across her naked buttocks, Caristia - unable to take her eyes from the uncontrollable dark-haired beauty - was overwhelmed by a sudden and unheralded orgasm.

Chapter 3
The Happy Phoenix

It was evening and the sun had just dipped behind the southern slopes of Vesuvius. Magnus led Caristia on a leash tied to a collar around her neck as they made their way to the Happy Phoenix, a rowdy bar at the junction of three roads which led only to the Amphitheatre. Its front was a typical L-shaped bar with large pots set into it to keep food hot. Behind this, a wooden rack for storing amphoras of wine and at the back of this three other rooms for guests - who could stay with female company if they required - a storeroom and a lavatory. Alongside the guest rooms was a large open courtyard with a fountain at its centre used to keep a small vineyard and for open-air drinking, eating and entertainment. Across the full width of the courtyard two heavy wires were suspended and on these were ranged recently lit candles set in flimsy brass holders. The outside wall, abutting the street, was covered in graffiti penned by the partisan supporters of various gladiators, all of whom passed this way on their journey to the arena, although only the victors returned. The innkeeper, Euxinus, often bought women from Rufo and used them for entertaining his guests then, when they were worn out, he sold them on as house servants or attendants at the arena. Euxinus's entertainments were well known in Pompeii and many of Rufo's customers were to be found at his hostelry.

Magnus pulled Caristia behind him as he ducked to enter the bar. Rufo strutted ahead looking from side to side to see if there was any chance of doing business as he had not sold a single slave since Fronto's last visit.

'Euxinus!' he shouted eagerly. 'Euxinus!' A stocky man with cropped grey hair and a grey robe tied at the waist with a sash, pushed his way through the noisy crowd of drinkers. 'Ale Euxinus. And something to entertain me.'

Euxinus looked straight at Caristia and was transfixed by her blonde beauty and pale, fragile demeanour.

'Olconio Rufo. You have brought me a special prize I see.'

Rufo laughed good-heartedly.

'She is not for you my dear Euxinus. I am training her for something very special.'

'You disappoint me Rufo,' Euxinus said, stretching out his chubby hand and fondling Caristia's pert breasts. 'I am sure she would have done well on my little entertainment evenings.' Magnus grabbed his wrist and pushed him back sharply. Euxinus turned to Rufo, shocked. 'Your freed slave asserts his new rights strongly Rufo.'

'Yes,' said Rufo. 'He still knows my wishes, and my wish for this young beauty is that you do not touch! Now! Entertainment. It is hot and I am dry. I have done no business yet today and am in need of something to lift my spirits.'

'I will not disappoint you Olconio Rufo. Look, arrived only yesterday a troop of Egyptian acrobats. The girls are fresh from Nubia, guaranteed virgins, and the boys are just, well my dear Rufo, they are just so beautiful.'

Three nubile young women with short cropped hair and two muscular young men sprang through the crowded bar and ran, all the time energetically leaping and tumbling, into the courtyard at the rear. Rufo pushed forward and Magnus snatched Caristia's lead. She winced as the leather collar pinched her neck then, enjoying the tension, allowed herself to be pulled forward until, dragged to the front of the crowd that now gathered around the courtyard, Magnus slackened the leash and it drooped limply across her breasts. As the soft leather glanced against her nipples, they hardened and pushed out the front of her thin tunic in two delightful peaks. She flushed slightly as two men turned and stared at them.

Everyone was enthralled by the acrobatic display and men in the crowd leered between the splayed legs of the young women, gawping at the tight-stretched panties of pure silk, as they extended their agile bodies to the limits in order to perform their feats. The male acrobats lifted the girls high above their heads, holding their legs apart wide then, to the gasps of the crowd, dropped them as if they would hit the floor, only to save them at the last minute and swirl them around by the ankles as their faces skimmed the delicately mosaicked floor.

Rufo cheered energetically as he drank glass after glass of lemon-scented wine and Caristia, sensing the rare feeling of freedom on her slack lead, edged to the front of the crowd. The two young men swished canes around the young women's ankles and they leapt to avoid them, then the girls stood on their hands, allowing their short tunics to fall around their faces and expose their tight panties and bare breasts. The crowd roared and Caristia edged even further forward.

Suddenly a sixth member of the troop leapt into the courtyard: He was dressed like the other two men; in only close-fitting tights, but instead of their lissom athleticism and beauty he was dwarfish, thickset and ugly. The crowd shouted with joy as, acting out a play, the dwarf chased the women, first somersaulting to show his skill then dropping onto all fours as he imitated a wolf chasing its prey. The three young women cowered in mock fear then, when the other two men came to their rescue the three women climbed onto their shoulders and formed a pyramid. They clutched each other, pulling their white tunics up to their faces and exposing their silky panties and one of them, her bare breasts. The dwarf stalked around them then swung round to the crowd as if turning his animal intentions elsewhere. Everyone gasped and backed off, then laughed loudly at their own stupidity. The dwarf lurched forward and grabbed Caristia's tunic. She shrieked in fright but, before the dwarf had time to do anything else, Magnus grabbed him around the waist and lifted him bodily into the air.

'Look how your freed man Magnus lifts the dwarf, Rufo!' exclaimed Euxinus excitedly. 'He is like Zeus with one of his children. The little man is like a toy to him. We should call the midget Minimus. Yes, Minimus!'

The crowd started chanting his new name as the dwarf struggled frantically to escape the clutches of his captor.

'Let him go Magnus. Let our little Minimus go free so we can see his performance,' urged Rufo.

Reluctantly Magnus lowered the dwarf in his massive hands and, as he set him down, he held him there and scowled at him. Minimus shook himself and squirmed then Magnus suddenly released him. Minimus carried on with his performance as if nothing had happened. He stalked around the women as, still clutching each other on the shoulders of the two men, they feigned fear. Suddenly Minimus sprang forward and snatched one from her perch. He dragged her to the floor and she twisted and turned, as if in a dance, as he reached and strained to keep hold of her. She dropped to the floor, sitting with one leg crooked up under her thigh and the other stretched out fully. Her cream panties pulled tightly across her splayed cunt and the slight hollows on the insides of the tops of her thighs opened the material slightly at the sides. As she sat there motionless with her head cocked back, it was just possible to see that she was completely shaved. Minimus prowled around her, still playing his part, sniffing at her, pawing at her, and each time he got close she drew back with an acted expression of fear and revulsion. Suddenly, as if angered, he made a grab for her and took hold of one of her ankles, but she pulled away and cowered on all fours behind the small fountain in the centre of the courtyard. Minimus ran around throwing his hands into the air with dramatised frustration before dashing into the bar and returning with a coil of rope. He stood on the fountain and spun the rope like a lasso, then flicked its frayed end at the woman catching her on the hip with its burning, snapping tip. She looked surprised, as if she had not expected it, as if it was not part of their act, then he flicked it again and she shouted out in obvious pain.

The crowd yelled for more and Minimus, egged on by their encouragement, leapt at the woman excitedly. He wrapped the rope around her ankle and, before she had time to pull it away, he yanked it tight and started pulling her across the floor. She screamed loudly as he dragged her around then, when her hands slipped and she fell onto her side, he handed the rope end to someone in the audience and dashed back into the bar to fetch another. The woman wriggled against the rope around her ankle, almost reaching down to it but, just as her straining fingers reached it, Minimus wrapped the second rope around her other ankle and pulled back on it until she fell over on her back and was splayed wide.

She threw her head from side to side and shouted out in a language no one could understand. '*Men fadlak saadni! Men fadlak saadni!*' she cried. 'Please help me! Please help me!'

Minimus knelt between her legs and leered at the crowd. They urged him on and, grinning and gyrating his hips, he wriggled his silky tights down over his stumpy legs. Minimus had a massive cock, both in itself and relevant to his otherwise diminutive size. It stuck out like a forearm from his groin, held out stiffly at right angles with heavy, pounding pulses, tensed and veiny and with a fist-like glans throbbing at its end. He held it in his hand and waved its incongruous bulk as though it was a staff. The crowd cheered and shouted loudly and the men holding the ends of the ropes pulled them even tighter and the young Egyptian woman, overcome by fear, shrieked continuously. Minimus pulled his hands up and down the length of his massive cock, causing the veins to expand and the pulsating tip to engorge even more. The crowd was in an uproar. He wriggled forward on his stumpy legs and knelt across her chest, first pressing the end of his cock against the sides of her face then forcing it tightly into her gaping mouth.

She tried to push him away but two men from the crowd ran forward with more rope, bound each wrist and pulled them wide until she was spread-eagled, as if on a cross, beneath the chuckling, red-faced Minimus. He lifted her head forward and drove his cock deeply into her mouth. She gagged and choked as it touched the back of her throat but he did not release her and held her there, his face reddening more all the time, as he pressed the massive shaft in between her tight-stretched lips. She closed her eyes tight and snorted through her nose until her cheeks bulged with the hugely expanding glans as he reared back and finished. He held her there, clamping her lips around his veiny cock, keeping it crammed in, forcing her to suck it and, not until she had swallowed it all, did he release his grasp on her and let her head fall back to the floor. She choked and moaned and his semen ran from the sides of her stretched mouth. Minimus looked at the crowd and grinned then, his cock still as stiff as before, he sprang up and leapt from her.

The men holding the ropes slackened them and, for a moment, thinking she would be freed, she sat up and started to wipe her face with the back of her hand. But, as she sat, looking hopeless and used, the two men ran across the courtyard holding the ropes, twisting her over as they took up the tension again and pulled her over violently, stretching her arms out again but, this time, face down. Her tunic was pulled up around her waist and her cream panties, although smoothed across her splayed cunt, were pulled deeply into the crease of her buttocks.

Minimus leapt across to the other members of the troop - the two men and two women - who were by now holding each other in fear. Minimus brushed the two men aside and caught hold of one of the women. She was slim and elegant, taller than the other one, with high cheekbones and wide, dark eyes and her pale skin hardly contrasting with her ebony tunic and silky panties. Her breasts were small and her dark nipples stood out erect beneath the material that covered them. Minimus twisted her around then, taking a rope offered to him from the crowd, he bent down to her ankles, coiled the rope around them several times and bound them together tightly. She tried to turn around, as if to ask the other acrobats for help, but Minimus tugged the rope and brought her to the floor heavily like a lassoed steer. She shouted at him and spat, pleading for mercy and showing her contempt for his apparent betrayal, but he took no notice.

Looping the rope that led from her ankles he tied her wrists behind her then, being careful to stop it tangling up in her tunic, he led it down the small of her back and between her taut buttocks. He pulled it between them until it could not be seen then wrapped it around her waist before once again bringing it between her athletic buttocks. She looked at him fearfully, biting her lips and shaking. He took a *fasces* and wedged it behind her knees then led the rope around several times until her legs were secured, splayed wide at the knees, to the *fasces*. Finally, he wrapped the rope around the centre of the *fasces* and knotted it tightly. She lay there, unable to move, completely at his mercy. He bent down and laid his head between her legs, licking the gusset of her panties with his fleshy tongue and darkening the silky material where it pulled wetly against the crack of her cunt. Suddenly, he jumped back and threw the spare end of the rope up over the two heavy wires that ran the full width of the courtyard. It draped over them and fell back, knocking the wires from side to side and causing a spray of hot wax to fall like a shower onto the courtyard.

Minimus dodged back to avoid the falling wax and his captive screamed as some of it splattered on her shoulder and cheek. She twisted sideways to avoid more and, as she did, Minimus tensioned the rope over the wires and yanked it hard. The *fasces* lifted and her body was twisted off the floor. Two men rushed forward and helped the dwarf pull, and to the excited screams of the crowd, they dragged the girl clear of the floor.

They hauled her higher and each time they pulled, the wires shook and wax sprayed down onto her. It fell first onto her shins and on the tops of her downturned feet, then as she got higher and it had less time to congeal, it ran from her knees and down the fronts of her thighs. She screeched to be released but her tormented screams only increased. Hot wax rained down on her, running along the insides of her thighs until it reached the tight gusset of her panties. It splattered against the material, each drop causing her to yell and twist, and each time she twisted the candles rocked more on the wires and released more of their wax. Finally, as she spun beneath the storm of wax, the two men tied off the rope. She whirled above them, twisting and turning and screeching with terror. Her tunic fell down over her face, baring her breasts and muffling her screams and, in a desperate act to try and stay the pain, she took the material into her mouth and bit it.

Caristia watched as Minimus climbed on someone's shoulders and began beating the woman with a bamboo cane. First he caught her across the buttocks, reddening them with thin bright stripes, then as she twisted on the rope he thrashed the sides and fronts of her hips, her back and finally, her breasts. Red stripes appeared everywhere he made contact and, as he thrashed her harder, Caristia saw the woman's dark nipples harden until they were themselves a sufficient target for Minimus's flailing cane. As she spun he brought it down across the hard nipples, aiming carefully, timing his blows and measuring them precisely so that as she revolved, bound and upside down on the rope, each received the same number of strikes.

The wax continued to spray onto her, running around the gusset of the panties that were stretched across her splayed cunt, flowing onto it, and running between the cheeks of her bottom before swirling out onto them and solidifying. Minimus beat her remorselessly, bringing the cane down harder with each stroke, cutting into the wax that had hardened, splashing the wax that was still hot. She twisted and turned then, with her tunic gripped tightly in her mouth and covered in the wax that continued to rain down on her, Caristia watched in amazement as the woman tightened and screeched with a sudden, fitful paroxysm of delight. The young acrobat's muscles tightened across her stomach and she lifted her hips to meet the cane as it came down hard against the wax-splattered gusset of her panties. She tightened her legs, straining to open herself to the source of the pain then, unable to stay the force of her flooding pleasure, she pulled herself up on the rope, curled forward and, with Minimus still flaying her, let out a massive screech of delight.

Caristia pulled forward and felt again the tension of the collar around her neck. She swallowed hard as it tightened and, as the young woman was lowered to the floor, still jerking with the convulsions of her orgasm Caristia saw the dissipated look of bliss on her sweat-covered face. Caristia pulled forward more and felt the moisture flowing against the inside edges of her fleshy, swelling cunt. She felt her lips drying as she peered closely at the woman's body, spattered with wax, striped red from the blows of the cane and gasping with uncontrollable spasms of her still flowing bliss.

Someone snatched the cane from Minimus and ran to the woman who was still stretched out, face down on the floor, with ropes attached to her wrists and ankles. He bent beside her, measuring the cane against her taut buttocks, touching them, patting them, rubbing the edge of the bamboo switch softly against her smooth pale skin. The cane bent as he held it in the indentation where her bottom met the tops of her thighs, then he moved it slowly across the gusset of her panties, stretched so tightly across the soft skin of her cunt. He poked the end of the cane at the cream panties which, as they curved towards the waistband on her hips, were pulled deep into the crease of her bottom. But the material was too tight for the thin cane to dislodge, like a second skin to her smooth, pink labia. He tapped the cane against her pert cheeks, testing her response, seeing how she responded to the lightest touch then he tapped harder, flicking his wrist to make the thin end of the cane snatch and bite as it contacted her. He stepped back, reaching down with his arm at full stretch, then swinging his arm fully behind his head, and pausing for only a moment, he brought it down hard. The loud swishing sound it made as it cut through the air ending in a sharp crack as it landed, burning her unmarked skin.

A red line, thin but harshly drawn against her pale skin, appeared straight away. It was as if the cane was covered in red paint and had stroked her with its colour. He brought it down again and Caristia watched it curving above his head, bending with the force of the stroke, singing with a swish of expectation before again it cracked as it landed on its taut target. The woman writhed, slowly as if she was trying to hold back the pain, but the next one, the third swishing stroke, the third reddening crack, made her lift herself against the strain of the ropes and twist her body in a vain, hopeless wriggle of suffering. The next one and all that followed left their own mark, each one drawing a precise red line, finding a fresh space to fill, a slightly different angle of approach, and each new stroke of the reddening brush, each new artistic line that was drawn on her, brought an increased squirm, a more desperate movement and a louder cry from the tortured, stretched out captive.

Caristia was leaning forward against the tension of her collar, drawing her knees together, massaging the wet outer flesh of her cunt, which moistened more with each stroke of the punishing cane. Her mouth dried and, as her hard nipples ached with longing she was filled with a flood of desire and need. Suddenly there was a commotion near to her; two men were fighting and Magnus tried to push them away from his charge. The tension on her neck was released, the leash dropped by her side and she fell forward, away from the protecting mass of the crowd and into the exposed centre of the courtyard.

The crowd roared excitedly as they caught sight of her pert breasts, pale Saxon skin, spiky flaxen hair and bright blue eyes. She stood, suddenly on display, unrestrained with the lead dangling from the leather collar at her neck. She looked around, breathing fast like a nervous fawn but, in truth, panting with excitement and seething with her boiling desires. She did not look back to see Magnus still struggling with the two men, as her ears, deafened for a moment by the baying of the crowd, filled again with the swishing cracks of the flailing cane as it continued to come down on the buttocks and now the back of the woman on the floor. Caristia could only see the red slashes on the young woman's body and she could only hear the snapping energy of the now split end of the cane released in burning crackles on the flesh of its writhing victim.

Caristia ran forward and the man wielding the cane stopped in surprise. She looked at the weapon in his hands and looked again at the woman on the floor.

Caristia lifted her tunic, wriggling it up around her neck then, as if crucifying herself, she lay face-forward, on the woman's back, stretching out her arms and legs rigidly, as if she too was held by the tensioning ropes that secured the woman. The man lifted the cane and Caristia sensed it, she pictured the woman's flesh scorched by the flail, now pressed against her own breasts and hips. She heard the swish as he brought it down, lifting her bottom, still covered by her panties and waited for the burning moment that would ignite the delectable pain of punishment.

Each crack of the cane brought her more delight, she rose up to it, lifting first her bottom until it was covered in thin red stripes, then her back, the backs of her thighs and finally - and only when she knew she was reddened everywhere and burning with the pain - she turned onto her back and lifted her hips for more. She kept her legs open wide, encouraging his aim towards her cunt, urging him to strike it hard then, when someone ran forward and tore her panties off, she stretched herself even wider so that she felt it on the fleshy edges of her swollen, aching slit. Someone pulled her tunic up over her face and, as she gasped in the darkness of its cover, her nipples were beaten until, still stretching her arms and legs wide, she began to feel the onset of her first orgasm.

It filled her as they ripped her garments away completely and, as a heavy, venous cock was forced into her mouth, her orgasm was finally released. She shuddered as her hips rose up and she sucked desperately on the cock as again, the cane beat down and she went rigid with pain, delight and the tension of her convulsive paroxysm. She cried out as semen flowed into her mouth and she gulped at it as they dragged her from the other woman and bent her forward on her knees. They thrust her deeply one by one, sometimes in the cunt and sometimes in the anus then they forced her to suck two cocks at a time while she was turned over and taken again. Hot wax fell onto her and she felt its stinging pleasure but as, taken again from behind and swallowing semen hungrily, she felt the swell of her repeated orgasms overcome her and she dropped forward exhausted.

Euxinus stepped out into the courtyard holding his hands out towards the female acrobats, urging the crowd to applaud as though he himself had performed some great feat before them. The two male acrobats ran forward eagerly and he took their hands and presented them to the crowd. The two young women, the one still trailing ropes from her ankles and the other rubbing the wax from her body with a towel, ran up together, smiling and laughing and bowing to their crowd of admirers. Everyone cheered and the Happy Phoenix filled with the howling roar of its satisfied onlookers.

Magnus lifted Caristia in his arms. She was still shaking from her ordeal. Semen dribbled from the corners of her mouth, strands of candle wax ran across her breasts and between her legs, and she was lined with red stripes from the thrashing she had received at the hands of the crowd. She looked up at Magnus through bleary, half closed eyes and briefly thought she saw him smile before the darkness, like a blessing against her anguish, overtook her.

As they left, with Rufo puffing behind them, a woman's well-manicured hand reached out from behind a purple curtain drawn across a small booth in the courtyard. It grabbed hold of Euxinus's arm, bracelets and rings flashing in the flickering candlelight, and he stopped and turned.

'Who was that man?' asked the haughty, cultivated voice from behind the still drawn curtain. 'The one who owned that young girl with the flaxen hair?'

'That was Olconio Rufo, madam,' he said nervously as she continued to hold onto his arm.

'I thought as much. I have heard he runs an interesting business.'

'Yes madam. He is a trader in women slaves and delights of the flesh, madam.'

'Yes, my husband's friend Lucretius Fronto has told me of him. Go to this

Olconio Rufo's house and tell him to expect a visit from Arria Sulla, wife of the senator Sulla and cousin of the Emperor Vespasian himself. Say I wish to do business with him.'

'Yes madam,' said Euxinus, obviously flustered by her presence. 'Straight away madam. Straight away.'

Chapter 4
Caristia and Innocenti are sold

'Magnus!' shouted Rufo as he rushed into the atrium flustered and upset. 'Magnus! Magnus! Where are you?' Magnus hurried up behind him, still struggling to buckle up the large leather belt at his waist. 'Magnus. At last. We are to have a visitor, the wife of a senator no less, and a cousin of the emperor - Arria Sulla! She will want to choose a slave for herself I expect; she will certainly want to see our stock. I hope we have something to please her. Her recommendation will be worth an audience with the emperor himself. I will ignore the reputation she has for being impossible to please. Magnus, bring out our ten best and make sure they are presentable! And that Innocenti, the one returned by Lucretius Fronto as too weak for his pleasures, see if we can get rid of her. Yes, perhaps her fragile charms will interest the lady.'

'What should I do with Caristia?' asked Magnus, still pulling at his belt.

'Keep her out of the way. She is not for sale.'

Moments later, Arria Sulla arrived in a decorated chair borne high by huge black Nubian slaves, each one naked except for a tight-pulled loincloth and a thick, buckled leather belt. One of them took her hand as she alighted. She was tall and elegant with dark black eyes, a penetrating stare and an authoritative, superior presence. Her dark auburn hair, pulled tightly from front to back, was encircled by a curtain of ringlets which ran around her forehead and, at the sides, hung down below her ears. Delicately worked flakes of gold were woven into the ringlets and trailed loosely down the side of her elegant neck, as if the precious metal was of such little value that it was left simply tangled in her hair like leaves, to blow away in the slightest wind. She stalked ahead of her slaves purposefully and entered Rufo's house.

Rufo rushed up to her, wringing his hands anxiously and speaking rapidly.

'Madam, greetings. Greetings, madam. Arria Sulla is most welcome in the house of Olconio Rufo. Welcome indeed.'

'Stop slavering man,' she said sternly in a sharp, slightly broken voice. I am not here to listen to your fawning. I am here to purchase a slave, a female, who will not only serve well but who has entertainment value of that special sort. Do you understand me?'

'Yes madam. Yes, yes. Oh yes madam,' he jabbered as he led her through the atrium and into the cool peristyle garden surrounded by a fine columned cloister. Behind the columns were ranged erotic, full sized statues, some of copulating groups and pairs and some of men with huge erections. The air was filled with the scent of lavender and basil. 'I have many fine slaves who would suit you exactly, all female. I only deal in females, some from Germany and the Nordic lands - tall and slim with fine breasts and slender hips - though they can be difficult to control. Some of my clients like that of course. I have slaves from the north coast of Africa - elegant black beauties with ravenous appetites, so smooth-skinned and full-lipped - a great favourite with the gentlemen, if you understand what I mean, madam. And some, the cream of my selection, from Nubia and Egypt are delicate and quiet with tastes so refined and rare they can provide bliss with only the faintest touch of their soft, exquisite hands. And their lips! Madam, their lips!'

She waved her hand and a chair was brought. A male Nubian slave stood on either side of her and two others hovered behind them, watching what was going on, mindful of her safety, trained to protect her at any cost. Behind one of the columns that supported the tile covered roof of the colonnade which surrounded the garden, crouched Caristia, naked from bathing, suddenly unsupervised and curious about the rich visitor.

Magnus led the women in and glowered at the Nubians. It was as if they challenged him with their controlled silence and resolved purpose. There were ten, all young and beautiful, all with their wrists bound behind them, all naked and all tied together with a rope that looped between the tight leather collars around their necks. Three Germans led the way, the tallest first with a mane of red hair and crystal clear blue flashing eyes; the other two auburn-haired and looking about them like captured beasts. Three intensely black girls followed, all shorter than the German women, heavier breasted with fuller hips and dark brown eyes. Then came three tall girls. They were slender with short dark hair and wide green eyes and, although they were dusky in complexion it was a much paler dark than the Nubians - a light brown, yellowish hue - and all their feline beauty was captured by its glow. Last, and tugging against the collar around her neck, was Innocenti, sent back by an indignant Fronto who had complained strongly of his dissatisfaction with her performance. Her dark eyes were sunken and her black hair was ragged and tangled. The Germans had pubic hair which had been carefully trimmed to reveal just the beginning of their cracks. The Nubians' pubic hair was cropped short in small stubbly patches and the Nubians were all shaved; not only their pubic hair but the hair under their arms and their eyebrows had been removed. The thin pink line of their cracks was easily visible between their slender hips and when they walked - laying their toes down first with each measured pace and linked together by the rope - they shone like bronze statues. Innocenti's pubic hair was untouched but it was insufficient to cover her crack, and the delicate edges of her perfectly shaped cunt stood out clearly against the pale skin of her thighs and stomach.

'How do they take to punishment, Olconio Rufo?' asked Arria Sulla.

'All my slaves are punished regularly, madam. They are used to the cane, the whip and the hand. Magnus, bring out the red-haired German!' He turned to Arria Sulla. 'A fine beauty I'm sure you agree, madam. Such stature, she is like Venus herself. Bend before your mistress!' he ordered.

The red-haired German bent over as if the action was an exercise, reaching down athletically to her ankles and grasping them tightly. Her taut buttocks were slightly open, exposing the dark circle of her anus, and below that the swelling edges of her cunt were pressed together and squeezed against the insides of her bottom.

'To your taste, madam?' asked Rufo.

'I want to see how she takes a thrashing before I give my opinion,' she said, reaching her hand back towards her Nubian slaves without looking. The one nearest her right shoulder stepped forward. 'I will let one of my mastiffs test her.'

The Nubian pulled something from his buckled belt. Rufo at first thought it was a sword and wrung his hands fearfully, then to his great relief he saw his fears were misplaced. The Nubian drew out a leather paddle, about the length of a man's arm, rounded at the one end into a robust handle and flattened at the other, to about the width of a man's hand and about half as thick as a finger. He rubbed the flat end against the side of his muscular leg, feeling its lateral tension, then still holding it against his leg, he bent it outwards to test its elasticity. It flexed stiffly, bending first only at the point where the handle met the flat part then, as he applied more pressure, the paddle itself reluctantly showed its suppleness.

Caristia pulled herself against the thick-ribbed column, and feeling its coolness and bulk she bent her right leg and pressed the inside of her thigh against the cool marble. She felt the soft skin of her body pressing against its immovable mass, and she felt its vertical ribs digging into her as she squeezed herself against it. She urged her hips forward, lifting the base of her stomach against the column and feeling the indentation of its ribs pressing against the front of her crack. A rib caught into the nick of her cunt, opening it slightly, tugging at it, threatening to expose her, to break open the tight-pulled flesh and bare her to its might. She moved sideways, just enough to let the contact with the indentation open her and, as she felt the coolness of the stone against the swelling edges of her inner petals, she moved sideways again and felt the slippery wetness of her own moisture on the unforgiving pillar. She hung onto it and swallowed heavily, then peeped further around the column to watch what was going on.

'Now we shall see if your words are true, Olconio Rufo,' said Arria Sulla, nodding to the Nubian with the leather paddle.

He stood behind the German woman, a pace to her left, and reached out the paddle to see if he was at the right distance. Its flattened end lay fully across both her buttocks with his arm at full stretch. He did not look at his mistress again but, just as he drew his arm back for the first strike, he glimpsed Caristia as she peered around the column. She pulled her head back sharply but straightaway peeped out again, more afraid she might miss the moment that the paddle fell against the buttocks of the beautiful red-haired woman than she was concerned for her own safety.

The black slave took the paddle back - knowing she was watching again - until his arm was stretched behind him. He bent his elbow slightly, to impart more power, and then brought it down heavily. It struck her buttocks exactly where he had intended, fully across both her cheeks, a palm's width above her fleshy crack. She grunted as the breath was knocked from her, and lurched forward and had to release the grip she had on her ankles to keep her balance.

Arria Sulla tossed her head back and sneered, already, dissatisfied.

'Harder!' she shouted. 'And keep them coming.'

The redhead gripped her ankles tightly as the Nubian, measuring the position for the next blow, again laid the paddle against her buttocks. He held it a little lower than the first, marked out already by a red patch only a little smaller than the paddle which had inflicted it. He took his arm back again, waited for a second, fixing his eye on the spot then, still aware of Caristia's gaze, he brought it down on his victim's upturned bottom. Again she exhaled with a low, stifled grunt and again she released her ankles to stop herself falling forward, and again, when he lifted the smacking paddle away, a red patch was painted on her skin, this time closer to her exposed cunt.

Caristia pressed harder against the ribbed marble column as she stretched to see the woman's reddening bottom. She felt the cold stone against the flesh of her cunt, her breasts, her stomach and, as she lifted her leg higher and allowed the pressure to open her crack, she felt its chilling hardness against the envelope of skin that covered her swelling clitoris. She pressed harder and the prepuce drew back, exposing the engorging glans and, as it touched the stone pillar, a shiver of fire penetrated her hips and ignited the hot flames of desire. When the Nubian brought down the paddle again, when she heard it smack loudly against the taut skin of the woman's buttocks, when she saw the reddening patch of skin it left behind as he drew it back, the heat in Caristia's cunt increased and she pressed herself as hard as she could against the column. She lifted her leg higher, opening her crack wide, exposing the satiny inner layers and the hard erection of her clitoris, rubbing herself against the ungiving marble shaft, lifting herself as the Nubian took the paddle back, waiting, then drawing herself down - pulling her clitoris against the stone - when he delivered the blow. When she heard the loud smack and the woman's breathless grunt, and she saw the bent victim knocked forward, Caristia squeezed her clitoris so hard against the column that she whimpered as wafts of pain ran through her sweating body.

'Tie her before she falls!' shouted Arria Sulla as the woman stumbled forward under the pressure of another blow.

One of her black slaves walked forward and bound the German woman's wrist tightly to her ankles with thin satin cords. He knelt in front of her; his tight loincloth almost against her face. When the next blow fell it smacked even louder and, unable to steady herself by letting go of her ankles, she was tipped forward and her face pressed against the Nubian's covered genitals. Caristia saw the outline of his cock swelling beneath the flimsy cloth and, unable to suppress her pleasure, she moaned, clawing against the marble column as she timed her panting groans to fit with the incessant smacks of the punishing leather paddle and the beating rise of the Nubian's slowly erecting cock.

Each blow that fell, each resounding whack of the leather paddle on the woman's tight skin, made Caristia's moans more insistent and each smack, each reddening, stinging thwack, made the Nubian's cock grow thicker and longer. Its tip pressed against the woman's face, lifting the material that contained it higher as its shaft stretched towards her gasping mouth. The thrashing continued and she gulped with every blow, her mouth finally falling onto the head of the throbbing cock. She sucked it in, pulling at the material that covered it, licking it and drawing at it until she had it lodged against the back of her throat. She was gagging on it, gulping and panting, rolling her eyes, absorbing the pain of the beating and, all the time, Caristia was clawing against the pillar, sliding her fleshy cunt against its carved ribs, pulling them wide, rubbing her clitoris against it and eventually feeling the welling fire of her orgasm as it began to flow inside her quivering body.

The leather paddle kept smacking down on the woman's bottom, reddening both her stretched cheeks. Then, as she opened her legs under the strain and as she dropped further forward into the Nubian's cock, it fell on the sensitive edges of her fleshy cunt. She no longer made any noise, she did not groan or grunt or shout or scream as the pains ran through her each time the paddle landed. She only gulped deeper, sucked harder, and bit harder into the stretched material that covered the cock that filled her mouth. Caristia, her eyes wide, pulled her open cunt against the pillar, and as the black slave on his knees reared up with a streaming orgasm and the German woman choked and sucked and swallowed the copious flow of semen that oozed freely through the stretched material of his loincloth, she drove her fingers into her vagina and dropped onto them with a shuddering orgasm. She squatted on her hand, letting her body throb on it, delivering her ecstasy into the palm, rubbing against it, feeling the wetness of it as she gasped with breathless bliss.

Arria Sulla lifted herself on her chair. Her face was slightly flushed and she had her right hand inside her dress, cupped around her left breast with her finger and thumb pinching the erect nipple.

'I do not want her,' she said hoarsely, pointing at the German woman who was being untied. 'But that one looks interesting. Though she is very frail.'

Rufo stood in front of Innocenti.

'That is her charm, madam,' he said fawningly. 'You may find her frailty endearing. She pleads for mercy even before she suffers any pain. Though perhaps, on second thoughts, you require something more sturdy.'

'Let me be the judge of that,' she replied sharply. 'Bring her to me. I want to see her more closely.'

Innocenti was untied from the line and brought forward. She smiled nervously at Arria Sulla then dropped her eyes. Arria Sulla smiled, as if suppressing a laugh, then snapping her fingers to get her attention, beckoned the young girl to her. Innocenti walked slowly, all the time looking down at her own shuffling feet.

'You are a pretty young thing,' said Arria Sulla, looking up and down Innocenti's naked body. 'Bring me a glass of wine. It is hot and I need refreshment.' Innocenti turned around and was handed a tray of wine at Rufo's anxious prompt.

'Madam,' he said, seeing Innocenti's shaking hands and fearing Arria Sulla's anger if disappointed, 'Magnus should not have included her for your approval. She had been sold to,' he hesitated, realising that too much truth might jeopardise any potential sale. 'Yes, I mean she has been sold to another and merely returned for some extra training. Not that she has been found unsatisfactory, you understand. It is just that, as I said madam, she suffers too easily. Now, take this fine Nubian, a virgin, and a—'

'Enough, Olconio Rufo!' snapped Arria Sulla as she waved to Innocenti. 'Serve me, girl.'

Innocenti approached her nervously, the silver tray shaking in her trembling hands. She looked up from her feet, and tripped at the join of two paved areas in the centre of the courtyard and the tray slid from her hands. It clattered on the floor, the blue glass containing the wine smashed and the bright liquid splashed everywhere. Innocenti dropped her head and waited, frozen by fear of what must now befall her. Caristia stared at the girl, her waif-like naked figure trembling as she stood isolated and exposed in the centre of the courtyard. Caristia felt anxious for her, yet at the same time that anxiety - borne on the tension of anticipated punishment - set new waves of excitement running afresh in her still writhing hips.

'Magnus! Magnus!' shouted Rufo. 'Take the girl away. She brings dishonour to me. Take her away!' Magnus stepped forward but, as he reached out to take hold of Innocenti's trembling arm, Arria Sulla sat forward on her seat.

'No. Let her approach. Her youth is beguiling and her fear has a certain charm.' She smiled at Innocenti but Innocenti did not dare look up. 'And, .my dear Olconio Rufo, surely you have ignored the fact that she must be punished for her carelessness.'

'Of course not, madam. Of course not,' said Rufo. 'I was going to suggest it myself.'

'Here girl. Come here. Lie across my lap,' said Arria Sulla, lifting her finely woven verdigris dress and patting her exposed knees. Innocenti moved slowly, biting her lips and rubbing her sweating hands against the fronts of her thighs. She stopped in front of Arria Sulla and looked up under her eyes. 'Yes, my child, bend over; you must be spanked for your sloppy service.' She waved her hand to her Nubian slaves and motioned them to position themselves kneeling and facing inwards on either side of her lap. 'Now my child. Here.'

Innocenti squeezed past the Nubian on Arria Sulla's right and stood facing her

34

bare knees. She glanced around quickly and saw Rufo, who nodded insistently for her to do as she was told. She bent forward and curled her naked body over Arria Sulla's lap. Her pert bottom rose, taut and pliant, her narrow back arched easily and her head hung down until her short dark hair nearly touched the floor. Arria Sulla smoothed her hands across the girl's back, tracing her fingers around her shoulder blades then along her spine, circling each vertebra until she reached the neat cleft of her buttocks. She paused there for a moment then ran her forefinger between the crack of Innocenti's bottom, wedging it in the delectable valley and drawing it slowly between her cheeks until she reached her dark, tight anus. She pressed the tip of her finger against it and Innocenti gasped, then as Arria Sulla pushed her finger in far enough to widen the muscular ring, Innocenti drew breath sharply and reared back. Arria Sulla removed her finger and smacked Innocenti's bottom.

'Stay still girl!' she shouted and smacked her again. Innocenti bent her legs, trying to protect herself with her raised feet, but the slave on that side pulled them down. Arria Sulla put her left hand in the middle of Innocenti's back to keep her in place then brought her hand down again on the girl's already reddened bottom. A loud smack brought a shriek from Innocenti which made Arria Sulla smile. She smacked her again, this time reiterating her victim's crimes and measuring the blows to fit with her oration.

'This is for stumbling and this for being too slow... and this for wriggling and this for crying out... and this...'

She stopped and listened to the girl panting and gasping, listened to her trying to hold back her screams, trying to fight back her tears. Arria Sulla grabbed Innocenti's hair and pulled her head back. Innocenti gulped loudly and choked.

'Please madam,' she muttered. 'Please.'

'Quiet girl!' shrieked Arria Sulla, overwhelmed with anger. She stared at the two Nubians on either side of Innocenti and her glower conveyed her desires. The one on her left pulled his loincloth away and held his hardening cock in front of the young girl's mouth. He lifted it between her open lips and held it there as it continued to grow and stiffen. 'Perhaps that will keep you quiet!' shouted Arria Sulla as she motioned to the other Nubian to remove his loincloth. He held his cock in his hand and presented it to the neat crack of Innocenti's cunt. 'Not there, you fool,' shouted Arria Sulla, wedging her hand between Innocenti's buttocks and exposing her tight anus. 'Here! Here!'

Caristia watched the first Nubian inserting the throbbing end of his cock into the girl's quivering mouth. She backed away from the pillar and, as the other Nubian pressed his cock against Innocenti's tight anus, Caristia felt her own bottom against the statue of a man that stood behind her. In unison with the cock that sank into the girl's anus, Caristia wriggled herself against the erect cock of the statue, opening her buttocks, positioning her anus against the sculptured tip then, as the black slave drove his cock in, and the girl's screech was reduced to nothing more than a blubbering, Caristia dropped herself onto the hard cock and took it in.

Arria Sulla starting spanking Innocenti again, timing her blows to fit the thrusts of the Nubians' cocks and confining her target to the nearest cheek of Innocenti's bottom. As the two men drove faster and the smacks copied their pace, Caristia thrust back harder onto the rigid cock of the statue, feeling the shape of its glans and every one of the carved veiny striations on its inflexible shaft. The smacks got louder and faster and the men's cocks drove deeper and Caristia pushed her fingers into her cunt as, with a crescendo of spanks both the Nubians finished explosively and Caristia screamed out loud. Semen burst from Innocenti's mouth, followed by her pent-up cries and, as the other Nubian drew his wet cock from her anus and its dark ring closed onto the oozing semen, Arria Sulla pushed the girl dismissively off her lap onto the floor. Caristia moaned and this time she did not go unheard.

She sagged to the floor, no longer bothering to protect herself from view, unaware of the glaring eyes that had fallen on her. The pale skin of her face was flushed and her hands, wedged between her legs, were wet and glistening with the moisture which had flowed so freely from her throbbing cunt.

Arria Sulla looked at her in amazement.

'Olconio Rufo! Are you master of your own house? Are you so slack with your slaves that they take their own pleasure whenever they please?'

Rufo, overwhelmed with embarrassment, wrung his hands and shouted at Magnus, as if passing the blame would somehow eradicate the fault.

'Magnus! Magnus! Magnus! Have you lost control of your charges? Magnus!'

Caristia, apparently oblivious to Arria Sulla's anger and Rufo's embarrassment, looked at the two Nubians still kneeling on either side of their mistress. She felt a wave of compassion for the hopeless Innocenti, now lying weeping on the floor, and it combined with an overpowering desire to take her place. She got to her feet and, naked and with her own wetness shimmering on the insides of her thighs, she walked towards them. Arria Sulla did not speak, she just watched as Caristia stepped around Innocenti, stood like a penitent before her, then turned sideways and folded herself gracefully over her bare knees. She stretched her head back, arching herself enough to put her face squarely in front of the cock of the kneeling Nubian, and parted her legs enough to make her anus visible from behind. Arria Sulla placed her left hand on Caristia's back and Caristia lifted her smooth bottom, opening the cleft between her buttocks wider and exposing the flesh of her cunt. She moaned as Arria Sulla pressed harder against her back and she opened her mouth as wide as it would go so she would be ready for the massive cock that throbbed in swelling beats in front of her face.

She moaned again and Arria Sulla motioned to the Nubian on her left. He edged forward and placed the throbbing glans between Caristia's stretched lips. It barely fitted. Caristia's eyes widened and her cheeks sank inwards as she started to suck. Arria Sulla told the Nubian on her right to wait, and he knelt behind Caristia, holding his cock in his hand, running his fingers along it, causing the tip to swell until he could barely close his fingers around it. Arria

Sulla rubbed Caristia's upturned bottom, massaging it, feeling its elasticity and, with each circular movement, Caristia sucked harder on the cock in her mouth and lifted her buttocks a little higher. Arria Sulla took a moment to pull her skirt higher, lifting it so that the shaved cleft between her legs was just visible. She looked upwards, as if ecstasy was to be bestowed on her, raised her right hand to just above head height, paused as her eyes flickered with anticipation, then brought it down with a loud smack on Caristia's bottom.

Smack followed smack as Arria Sulla spanked Caristia, harder and faster with each strike. Caristia sucked earnestly, feeling the swollen cock against the insides of her cheeks, drawing it to the back of her throat, swallowing it. She rode each stinging smack, lifting herself against it as it fell, wriggling beneath it as the scorching pain ran through her, opening her buttocks to expose herself for the next, all the time being lifted, as if by angels of pain and submission, towards a heavenly bliss.

Arria Sulla drew her left hand up between her own thighs and probed her fleshy cunt. She opened her legs a little and still spanking Caristia hard, pushed her fingers inside the delectable warmth of her own flesh. She licked her dry lips as she watched Caristia sucking the hard cock, then as she saw the girl's passion driving her towards a climax she signalled to the slave on her right. He held his cock out, rubbing it with his own spit, then levelled it against Caristia's dilating anus. He pressed it a little and it was immediately sucked in, its veiny bulk squeezed tightly at the entrance and compressed by the clenching flesh within.

Caristia reared back as the cock sank into her anus, she sucked even harder on the one in her mouth and, as the spanking hand of Arria Sulla fell repeatedly on her left buttock, she tightened like a spring and convulsed with a massive, shuddering orgasm. The spanking continued and she reared up again as she felt a hot flow of semen in her throat, then as she sucked it down, swallowing in thirsty gulps, she tightened again as she felt the heat of a second flow spurting deep into her rectum. She rode the cocks, squirming between them as if she had been secured to a pole, all the time taking the spanking that Arria Sulla dispensed. Only when the spanking stopped, only when the cocks were drawn from her and she lay, dissipated and gasping, semen dripping from her mouth and from her open anus, did the throbbing of her ecstasy begin to subside.

Arria Sulla took her fingers from between her legs, bent to Caristia and stroked her sweat-soaked hair. 'This is the one I want, Olconio Rufo. This flaxen-haired beauty is my choice. I have never seen one so eager, so determined to seek out pleasure.'

'But madam, madam, she is not...' he paused nervously and opened his eyes wide. 'She is not, madam, for sale.'

Arria Sulla ignored him as if his comment were beneath contempt.

'There is no need to entertain me further, my friend. Do not tire yourself with joking. I realise she will need some work, but I am prepared to put it in. I will take her directly. I do not want her to be an expense to your household any longer. Send a note of the price to my secretary. I am staying at Fronto's summer villa on the edge of town; the House of the Amorini. Good day. I have enjoyed my visit.'

She got up, wriggled her dress down, regained her composure and walked across the courtyard into the atrium. A slight breeze caused the flakes of gold in the ringlets of her hair to tremble and reflect flickers of light across her high, smooth cheekbones. 'Oh, and I will take the young dark-haired one as well. Not that I think she is worth anything, but to save you from the embarrassment of her, and all the trouble of further training. Pay her owner off. I am sure that whoever it is will not miss her.' She tossed her head back and laughed. 'Leave both their collars on. You can add the cost to your bill.'

Chapter 5

The brothel of Queen Isis

The House of the Amorini was a fine building on the Road of the Tombs, nearly at the Herculaneum Gate. It had an open terrace, a large atrium with a fountain, and a grove at the rear where peaches and nectarines flourished above a cooling, covered walkway. It was much finer than Rufo's house, and Caristia was wide-eyed at the sight of the bright mosaics, rich furnishings and stylish decoration. In keeping with its name, cupids and cherub-like amorini were carefully portrayed in all the main rooms, naked and plump, entwining themselves with ardent lovers and offering their services, whatever they might be, for the pleasure hungry sweethearts they surrounded.

After they left Rufo's house, Caristia was kept separate from Innocenti and, although she saw her for the first few nights - when the rings in their collars were clipped into chains in a dark dungeon - she did not see her at the House of the Amorini again. To start with Caristia was made to serve at meals, but as Arria Sulla invited more guests to her lavish dinners Caristia was used increasingly as a source of pleasure. Often she was displayed naked - her pubic hair shaved on the instructions of her mistress, who said she would have none of her slaves any other way - her smooth skin gleaming with golden oil and white fragrant flowers in her blonde hair.

Sometimes she was dressed according to the theme of the evening or simply at the request of one of Arria Sulla's new friends. Once she was dressed as a nymph with gauzy fabric covering only her hips, and with small gold clips attached to her painted nipples. She had to drape herself backwards over the guests' knees and let them squeeze the clips tighter until she screamed. Once she was daubed in gold paint and made to perform in a play with dwarfs who took the parts of amorini and cupids. They tied her ankles to a rope and she was suspended from the ceiling while they licked the paint off. Once she was wrapped in sable fur and had to be hunted by the Nubians. When finally they captured her they pinned her down to the ground - spreading her wide by tying her wrists and ankles to stakes - before beating her with whips and riding crops. If at any time any of Arria Sulla's guests wanted to cane her or spank her she was always made available. Sometimes she would be taken over their knees, sometimes made to bend over a chair and sometimes tied up so tightly she could hardly breathe. Once she was tied to a fountain in the centre of the atrium and caned by all the guests, then after they had gone she was left there until the next evening when she received the same treatment. Once, because she had combed her mistress's hair badly, she was beaten with an oxhide thong in front of the guests by Arria Sulla's private slave flogger. On one occasion she had to attend one of the guest's wives who was herself spanked in front of everyone else because her husband objected to her sucking one of the male slave's cocks without asking his permission. Caristia was made to bend on all fours while the woman bent across her, then when the woman had been sufficiently punished they changed around and Caristia was spanked as well. Several guests to the house were priests at the Temple of Isis - what some of the other slaves called 'the brothel of Queen Isis' - and Arria Sulla fell into long conversations with them. In the end, under the spell of their winning arguments, she agreed to go to their place of worship.

Caristia followed Arria Sulla, borne high on the ornate chair by her Nubian slaves up the gradually sloping Road of the Tombs. It was getting dark but still very hot and the Nubians' oiled bodies were covered in glistening sweat. They passed a house with a large hanging balcony, then several brothels until finally, after passing Rufo's house and his slave quarters, they arrived at a brightly decorated temple enclosed by a high, lavishly painted boundary wall. The Temple of Isis had been built nearly a hundred years before for the worship of an Egyptian goddess, brought from the Nile by the armies of Marc Anthony, and co-opted, like so many other pagan gods from distant shores, into the complex mosaic of Roman worship. In the centre of the walled enclosure, approached by seven steps, the temple itself was an imposing stone building with a colonnaded entrance and a high-pitched roof. On the left of the open area in front of the steps - where most of the worshippers gathered - was a stone altar and above this, hanging from a large timber tripod, a closely braided rope with a pulley block at its end.

It was dark when they arrived and the walled enclosure was illuminated by fires which burned around its edges. Worshippers gathered in the enclosure and three men dressed in white and purple cloaks, each holding a gold chalice stood on the steps. Arria Sulla's Nubians cleared a path for her through the crowd and Caristia squeezed through in their wake, struggling to squirm between the tight-packed bodies of the chanting devotees, frightened in case she should get lost. She stood by the altar as Arria Sulla craned her neck to see what was going on.

Two pale-skinned young women, flanked by four Nubian boys, were being led out of the temple. Purple cloaks, held together at the women's throats by golden clasps, were draped over their shoulders. One was blonde and one dark-haired, but they were both blue-eyed and frail looking. The dark girl was made to stand at the top of the steps, where her arms were pulled around one of the columns and tied securely with rope. The other girl was turned around slowly by the Nubian boys, displaying her to the worshippers at the command of the priests as they sought the devotees' approval of her youth and purity. Her short blonde hair shone in the flickering light of the burning fires, and her smooth skin picked up the rosy glow of the flames as if she was surrounded by iridescent butterflies. Caristia pushed further forward between the chanting, tight-packed crowd but they were so crushed into the enclosure that she could not get any closer to the altar. She stood, squashed between several men, their hot bodies pressed against hers as she struggled to see.

Led by the three priests in robes, the blonde-haired girl was guided by the boys down the steps of the temple. The crowd parted as the priests moved through them, carving a path from the steps to the altar and crushing the crowd even tighter together. Caristia felt the men's bodies squashed even closer, pushing her, not only because of the pressure of the crowd, but through a desire to touch her, to feel her, to squeeze closely against her. She felt their hot breath on her face and neck and, when the crowd surged forward to fill the space behind the short procession, she felt two hands encircling her breasts.

The young woman was led to the altar and stood at one end. Her blonde hair glistened as the clasp at her neck was unclipped and the purple cloak removed from her shoulders. She stood naked and still with her hands by her sides as if she were frozen at attention. She was slim with small breasts and narrow boyish hips, and her face was pale and expressionless. Her pubic hair had been shaved and the crack of her cunt was clearly defined as a sharp pink slit. The priests held their chalices high, offering them to their mistress Isis, then in unison they turned and nodded their heads to the attendant boys. The hands around Caristia's breasts tightened their grip as the boys, supporting the girl under her buttocks, shoulders and calves, lifted her bodily and raised her above the altar. She was so slim that stretched out between them her hips stood up sharply above the shallow dip of her stomach, which led smoothly to the raised mound that sheltered her youthful crack. The hands tightened more around Caristia's breasts as fingers and thumbs began pinching her hardening nipples.

The boys laid the girl down on the cold stone altar. Caristia raised herself up on her toes to look over someone's shoulder and, as she lifted herself she felt a hand between her legs from behind, one of the priests stood by the side of the girl and lowered the ornate chalice, then chanting a prayer he tipped it and ran its contents - golden olive oil - across her breasts. It shone like liquid fire as it ran from the lip of the cup, then changed its form and flowed down in a golden stream of fluid silk as it folded around the girl's nipples and breasts. She parted her lips slightly as if inhaling the scent of the heavenly sap, and as Caristia saw her gasp slightly she felt her own wetness of her swelling cunt. The worshippers went quiet as the priest massaged the oil into the girl's skin, and

Caristia watched spellbound as the girl's nipples hardened and rose into two prominent erect peaks. The hand between Caristia's legs turned so that the palm was held just below the hot flesh of her cunt.

When the priest had rubbed the oil all over the girl's breasts he stepped back and the second one took his place. Again he held his chalice high then, chanting prayers, he lowered it and began emptying the contents over the girl. Again golden oil flowed, this time running across the girl's navel, into the hollow of her stomach, then as it gathered in a warm golden pool, flowing around the base of her stomach and into the tight crack of her sex. The priest rubbed the oil in, using the flat of his hands to embrocate the girl's body, covering again her breasts and teasing her hard nipples, then smoothing it over her stomach until finally spreading it carefully into her cunt. He ran his fingers along the glistening slit, opening it enough to expose the darker pink of its inner flesh, and then he let his hands move down, massaging the insides of her thighs, her legs and her feet with the syrupy lotion. As he stepped back Caristia felt the hand between her legs rising towards the flesh of her own cunt, then as the second priest made way for the third, the hand pressed flatly against her engorging labia.

The third priest nodded to the boys and they lifted the girl again. Golden drops of oil dripped from her body, as if she were a sculpture of ice thawing in the heat of the flickering fires. They turned her over and laid her face down on the altar. The priest held his cup above her pert buttocks and, as the others had done, ceremoniously tipped the oil over the shallow lip. It ran first in a trickle, dribbling on the highest points on the delectable curves of her bottom and then, as he tipped the cup further, in a fuller, velvety flow that poured eagerly down both slopes, upwards into the small of her back and down onto the tops of her thighs. It gathered in the tight valley that lay between the cheeks of her upturned buttocks, then as if unable to resist the sweet flesh of her cunt, it sought out the inviting divide that lay squeezed between them. The priest massaged it in, running his fingers in circles across the girl's back and the backs of her thighs before smearing it over her buttocks, at first singly and then together. He probed his fingers deep between the crack so that he rubbed satiny balm around her dark anus, and then the soft flesh that was the raised edge of her cunt. As he nodded again to the boys the flat hand between Caristia's legs pressed up harder against her flesh, pinching and squeezing until she felt a shiver of pain.

Caristia licked her dry lips as one of the boys placed a long cane into the priest's hand. The fingers that squeezed her increased their pressure, catching the tip of her clitoris - already uncovered and erect - and sending a wave of heat throughout her whole body. The priest waved the cane above his head and whipped it from side to side in the flickering red light of the flames. Its tip was thin but even when he flicked it threateningly with his wrist it barely bent. The crowd of devotees quietened until Caristia could hear only the swishing of the cane as it whipped from side to side. She listened to it cutting the air with a menacing hiss and opening her legs, lowered herself onto the probing hand and let its fingers penetrate her.

The priest nodded again to the boys, who took up position at each corner of the altar. Two of them bound hide thongs around the girl's wrists while the other two held her ankles shoulder width apart and bound an ebony bar between them. They pulled the trailing ends of the thongs down the side of the altar and tied them into bronze pegs that were fixed to the sides. The girl's oily body shone in the shimmering light, her pert buttocks the golden apex of her glistening beauty. The two boys at the top end of the altar lifted her head and opened her mouth. Caristia saw how wide her eyes were and, in their fixed stare, she sensed her fear. The boys presented the girl's open mouth to a leather ball with thongs attached to each side, and after struggling to get it between her lips and behind her teeth they secured the thongs around the back of her neck. The two boys then drew a black leather hood over her face and they all stepped back.

Caristia moaned as the fingers probed her, then she felt a hand on her back and she was pushed forward, bending her at the hips until her bottom stuck out. She could still see the girl on the altar, but now it was more difficult. She stared at the motionless figure, bound, gagged and hooded, as the fingers delved deeper inside her wet cunt, and a hand lifted the hem of her short tunic and smoothed its palm across her bare bottom. The priest stood back and laid the cane across his victim's upturned buttocks. A sliver of oil covered its lower half and, when he raised it high above his head, droplets of the golden juice sprinkled from it like a shower of flickering gems. There was complete quiet as he held the cane high, waiting for the right moment. That perfect moment of action when he saw the girl's hard nipples rise higher as she breathed in slightly. When he saw the hood over her face suck in against her nose, or when he saw the glistening skin of her bottom twitch with a phantom pain brought on by anticipation of the real pain to come.

Caristia waited as well; the only thing that moved was the hand on her bottom. She pressed against it, hoping it would lift away, hoping it would copy the cane the priest held above the girl, hoping the crowding worshippers around her would clear away sufficiently for the hand to swing fully at her waiting cheeks.

Everyone around the altar gasped when the cane came down, it was so forceful, so penetrating. But when it struck the girl's bottom, when the swishing rod made contact with her flesh, she did not twist in agony, or writhe beneath its burning stroke. She was fixed too tightly to move, tied down too securely to lift herself to it or attempt to wriggle away. Only the side of the mask over her head showed that she gasped - her mouth plugged as it was by the leather ball - through the flared nostrils of her nose. The hand was not on Caristia's bottom any longer, but the blow had not arrived, it had not smacked her waiting skin, and she writhed back against the fingers in her cunt, frustrated by the abandonment, disappointed by the lack of much needed pain. She dropped forward, hoping to bring down the smack she yearned for and she lifted her bottom higher, opening the cheeks, exposing herself more. Still the fingers probed her, still they squeezed her soft outer flesh, and still they pinched ever more harshly on the throbbing hardness of her engorged clitoris. But still she could only wish for the palm of the hand to come down on her buttocks and she felt herself dribbling with a desperate, unsatisfied desire.

The priest brought the cane down again and a spray of golden droplets showered from its flaying length. The stinging blow striped the girl's bottom, even beneath the absorbent covering of oil, and when he lifted it away everyone could see precisely where it had landed. He took it back and brought it down again, another stripe of red, another spray of glossy oil, and again, and again until he was thrashing her continually, striping her bottom, her thighs and her back. Each stroke left its mark, but never in the same place, always somewhere different than before, always somewhere fresh, somewhere not yet sensitized by the pain, somewhere not yet marked by the thrashing staff of fire.

Suddenly Caristia heard a loud smack. Before she felt it on her buttocks she heard it, then as she widened her eyes with delectable surprise, the smarting pain followed and she moaned loudly with joyful relief. She bent forward more, tightening her buttocks and presenting herself fully for the next, then when it came, when it smacked loudly against her still stinging skin, the palm of the hand caught not only the reddened skin of her bottom but her exposed cunt. She dribbled profusely as the biting pain shot through her, as the vigour of the blow ran riot throughout her body, but she did not wriggle away or squirm to escape; she needed the pain and lifted herself up for more.

As she watched the cane being passed to the next priest, who took up the beating of the bound girl, the hand continued to smack her bottom. She reached down to the floor, stretching herself before the punishing hand, sacrificing herself to it, delivering herself up to its discipline. She could not see the girl on the altar any more, and now she did not try to look up. She could hear the stinging blows raining down on the girl's still body and she could sense the penetrating pain they delivered. Now the swishing sound of the cane and the cracking contact with another new place on the girl's exposed skin was enough to fill her. Her head was crammed with it and her mind was ablaze with the pictures it conjured up. She bent further and licked the ground. The earth tasted so good and she buried her face into the soil, spreading her tongue onto it and feeling it sticking to her lips. Suddenly she stopped, aware of a silence, the hand no longer spanking her and the cane no longer striking the girl. Caristia lifted her face and, resting on her elbows, she listened. She knelt on all fours peering vainly between the sea of legs that surrounded her. She got up, wiping her face and licking her lips, and gazed between two men that stood in front of her, clawing their shoulders to get a better look.

The blonde girl was left tied to the altar as the boys climbed back up the steps and released the dark-haired girl from the column. Her arms dropped by her side, she looked fatigued and hopeless, but the boys took hold of her straight away, first pushing her forward then lifting her, facing down, high above their heads. The crowd of worshippers dropped their heads as though they were praying - as if some offering had been made - then some men came forward with a heavy wooden cross joined into the shape of an 'X'. They fixed it at right angles to the altar, dropping the lower diagonals with a heavy thump into holes carved into the stone surface. The Nubian boys carried the girl down the steps, the hard nipples of her small breasts pointing downwards and her black hair dropping about the sides of her face. When they got to the cross they turned her upside down and placed her, face forward, against the freestanding structure. They splayed her legs wide and secured her ankles with leather thongs to the two diagonal uprights. They bound two more thongs around her thighs, halfway between her knees and her groin, then pulled a wide leather belt tight around her waist to hold her fast against the centre of the frame. She hung there for a while, her arms hanging loosely, her hands almost reaching the ground and her head lolling from side to side. One of the priests came forward and licked her naked cunt, drawing his tongue along the crack slowly from back to front, then while he stood back and gazed at the glistening valley of her flesh, the boys secured her arms to the lower diagonals, binding them securely at the wrists and upper arms.

Caristia stared between the girl's outspread legs as the boys massaged oil into her skin. It ran in golden droplets into the shallow hollows on the insides of her thighs that led to the exposed mounds on either side of her naked cunt. Caristia lifted herself up on the men's shoulders and could just see that some of the oil ran along the girl's sex, and the pinkness of her soft flesh gleamed with the redolent liquid. Some ran down between the crack of her bottom and down into the small of her back, between her shoulder blades then into the black hair, causing it to shimmer in the light of the fires. The oil dripped, and as it gathered in a small pool beneath her head it reflected back the redness of its light onto her shoulders and her upturned breasts.

Gaping and dry-mouthed, Caristia stared at the glistening body of the girl, her face turned between the diagonal bars of the cross, her limbs fixed tightly to its unyielding frame, her plight sealed. Caristia clawed up onto the men's shoulders again but they shrugged her off, keen themselves to see what was going to happen next. She craned her neck as she felt again the hand on her bottom, and she opened her buttocks to it, lifting herself onto her toes at the same time, as this time fingers probed around her anus. She squirmed around the fingers and one of them penetrated the muscular ring. As it went inside her she sensed a hollowness of excitement in her stomach and gasped, unable to absorb its pressure without a shock of delight. She took her eyes off the girl for a moment, losing her focus as her lids closed, then asserting herself against the overpowering sensation that flooded her, she pushed down onto the thrusting finger, allowing it to penetrate her fully. She gulped hard as she twisted herself onto it, squirming around it while, at the same time, holding onto the shoulders of the men in front of her so that now she should not lose sight of the crucified girl.

One priest moved behind the cross while another stood facing the girl's back. Caristia writhed on the finger, drawing it deep into her anus, then tightening the muscular ring to keep it there. The priest behind the girl knelt in front of her face, lifted his robe and exposed his hard cock. He held its throbbing end against her lips while the priest on the other side held out his hand and took a *fasces* from one of the attendant boys. He held the bundle of canes high behind his shoulder, then as the first priest inserted his cock into the girl's mouth he swept it down onto her upturned buttocks. She gulped the cock in as the blow fell, sucking hard to stave off the pain, filling her mouth with it to prevent herself from crying out. Caristia pulled herself up high, drawing herself up on the finger until the ring of her anus closed tightly behind the knuckle. She licked her lips, already feeling a swell of joy building somewhere deep between her hips. The priest wielding the *fasces* bought it down again and the girl sucked harder, then when it came down a third time, and her body tightened against the stinging blow, the first priest withdrew his pulsating cock, stood up and let his spurting semen run down onto the naked crack of her cunt. As it ran along the fleshy furrow it poured into the crevice of her buttocks and the next blow that came down onto them splashed it across the taut cheeks of her bottom.

Caristia watched a worshipper from the crowd taking the first priest's place, kneeling in front of the girl then lifting his robe and pushing his hard cock into her open mouth. The *fasces* continued to whip her buttocks, and because she was upside down, catching the tender underpart of her thighs, reddening them, lining them, striping them with evidence of its pain. Each time the bundle of canes struck her body tightened and she drew the cock in her mouth deeper, then inflamed by the jolting sucks of the agonized girl, the man's orgasm overtook him and, as he withdrew his cock and sprayed his overflowing semen across her cunt, the thrashing bunch of canes again spread it in glistening, creamy strands across her burning flesh.

Caristia rode the finger in her anus but it was not enough; the scene of suffering was inflaming her, setting her on fire, drawing her beyond any ability she had to control herself. She clawed up on the men's shoulders, squirming herself free of the delving finger, and watched another man kneel in front of the girl. As she saw him press his hard cock into the gaping mouth and watched the girl tensing again and again, as the blows rained down on her semen smeared bottom, Caristia pushed the men aside and rushed forward through the crushing crowd. As if emerging from a cave she broke out into the area in front of the altar, wide-eyed and dazzled by her exposure. She dodged to the side as two of the attendant boys ran towards her. She felt their hands on her arms but easily slipped their grasp. She chased towards the girl on the cross and stood in front of her splayed legs. A man was just spraying his semen onto the girl's vagina, already streaming wet with the ones that had gone before, and as he held the pulsating shaft and allowed it to pour its fluid onto the delectable flesh, Caristia

45

bent and started to lick.

All she could think about was the taste of semen and she licked like a hungry animal, spreading her tongue flat against the naked crack, lapping up the sticky semen and swallowing it in thirsty gulps. It spread across her face, congealing around her mouth and sticking in strands across her cheeks, and she forced her tongue deep into the girl's sex to get it all. Then the *fasces* swept down again. The swishing wind lifted Caristia's hair slightly, like a zephyr heralding the arrival of a god. Then the jolt as it hit the girl's buttocks ran through Caristia's body as if she had been struck herself. The extra tension in the girl's body only increased Caristia's thirst and she delved her tongue as deep as she could and rubbed her face against the sticky flesh. Another blow fell, then another, each one only increasing Caristia's need for more. Yet another one fell and in uncontrolled desperation Caristia held on to the girl's legs, bearing her face down, holding her tongue in the girl's cunt, licking, slurping, waiting for the next.

Another man knelt and fed his cock into the girl's mouth, then when he pulled it out and held it above the girl's open cunt, Caristia turned her face and took his semen directly on her tongue. She licked it away from the pulsating end, taking the full flow greedily, then she encircled the flanged rear of the glans with her lips and sucked hard to draw out every drop. She swallowed it all as the *fasces* swished past her cheek and struck the suffering girl on the buttocks. Caristia drew herself off the cock, satisfied she had taken it all, rubbed her breasts between the girl's legs then stood upright before the priest with the cane. She glistened with semen and sweat, and some of the oil from the girl's body ran down between her breasts into her navel. She held her arms up and spread them out at the same angle as the cross, then she spread her legs as well. She was offering herself in the girl's place, and the very thought of what she was submitting to ignited fresh fires of raging delight deep within her heated body.

The priest placed the *fasces* on the floor and ordered the girl to be untied. Caristia stood waiting as she was released, then as soon as she had been laid against the side of the altar she was lifted and bound in her place. As the boys pulled the thongs of leather tightly around Caristia's wrists she lifted her eyes with excitement, then when they fixed her ankles and she found she could not move her arms or legs, a shivering pulse of delight erupted within her. She gasped as it ran through her body, then when the belt was tightened around her waist and her forearms and her thighs were secured as well, she felt an orgasm burning through her like a raging firestorm. She could not lift herself up in response to it - because of her constricting bonds she could not twist herself to absorb it - and the suppression of her need to convulse, to jerk as it overtook her, made its power all the greater. But held in, bound inside her, this raging inferno of bliss did not exhaust her, did not deplete her energy, it only invigorated her, only nourished her and prepared her for more. Blood ran to her head and she felt her face burning as the first cock was pushed into her mouth. She took it all, sucking it and drawing it to the back of her throat, then as the *fasces* struck her upturned bottom she gulped it further, feeling the swollen glans at the top of her throat, which closed around it, an involuntary action, and she felt the throbbing tip expanding as her own grip tightened, then as the *fasces* came down again and she felt the burning sting against her skin, she tasted the onset of the gushing semen running already up the veiny shaft of the pounding cock.

She knew it was flowing over her cunt because she could hear the sound of the smacking *fasces* change. She knew it was splashing the semen all over her as it ran copiously between her reddened buttocks, but she could not concentrate on it; she was too ravenous, too eager to feed. She took another one in her mouth - a huge throbbing cock - and another even bigger and, as the beating continued and she felt the wetness of semen running down her body, she was enveloped in a haze of pain, delight and continually growing desire. The pain of the *fasces* was like a lover's kiss, the cocks in her mouth like ambrosia and the flow of semen - that soaking balm which now ran from her naked cunt down between her shoulder blades, under her armpits and finally up the side of her neck, her face and into her hair - was like a shower of heavenly rain. Orgasms ran through her with every blow, she was inexhaustible, but still none of them spelled the end, none of them quenched her desire or exhausted her ardour. Each throbbing pulse only inflamed her raging passion, only drove her to increased gluttony and she sucked harder and revelled in the thrashing until, at last, what had become a misty haze of ecstasy was finally overtaken by the shadow of blissful unconsciousness.

But it was a momentary darkness and she bit her lips and breathed in deeply though her nostrils as she felt herself being untied from the cross and placed on the cold stone of the altar. She felt the bonds around her wrists and ankles being tightened into the pegs on its side, and she heard the swish of the cane as it swooped down on her bottom. She welcomed the ball as it was forced into her mouth and she closed her eyes as the hood was drawn over her head and everything was cast into darkness. She rose up against the thrashing cane, responding to each strike as if it was the first, lifting her buttocks to meet it every time. She gasped as the blows got harder and she tightened with the rush of a renewed orgasm. When she was untied and the hood removed she rolled over, allowing the cold stone to ease her burning bottom, and she looked up at the pulley block as it swung above her like an ominous pendulum. It hypnotised her, swaying from side to side, and she wondered what delights it held, what punishment it was part of and although she could hardly dare to think it, if she would ever suffer from its use. She stared at it as the cane came down across her breasts and she watched it until darkness descended again.

Arria Sulla told one of her Nubian slaves to carry Caristia back to the House of the Amorini. She lay limply in his massive arms and smelled the strong tang of oil and sweat that came from his black skin. She inhaled it as if she were smelling the sweetest flowers and, as he carried her naked and sore body through the streets, she felt again the heat of excitement growing in her cunt. She looked up at the entrance to Rufo's house and the sign of the Happy Phoenix, then as they approached the Road of the Tombs and she saw again the overhanging balcony they had passed earlier, she pictured in her mind the swinging rope with the pulley held above the altar on the timber tripod. She imagined it swaying above the place where she had felt such overwhelming pleasure and, as she tried to think what it was for, she again remembered the stinging heat of the *fasces* on her bottom and the semen in her mouth. She realised she would be punished more when she was returned to the house, and she rose up in the Nubian's arms as she tightened with a final paroxysm of bliss.

Chapter 6

Caristia meets Drusus

Caristia walked obediently behind Arria Sulla's Nubians as they carried their mistress high along the road to the Sarno Gate. She did not look up at the Happy Phoenix as they passed the rowdy crowd at the doorway but, when they entered the grounds of the gymnasium, she could not keep herself from staring. Everywhere on the huge square arena, surrounded on all sides by long colonnaded walkways, were naked young men. Some were running or hurdling, some threw javelins, some wrestled or boxed and some simply stretched their oiled, muscular bodies in the warm sun. A large swimming pool at the centre was host to naked men diving and challenging each other to swimming races. Caristia felt a surge of warm wetness in her vagina merely at the sight of them. When she followed her mistress across the training ground, weaving between the juvenile gods, inhaling the scent of their oiled skin and their youthful musky tang, her nipples hardened and she felt the trickle of an orgasm running deep within her.

Seemingly oblivious of the activity that surrounded her, Arria Sulla led the party to the opposite colonnade where one of her Nubians brought her a chair. She sat down and lifted the hem of her skirt - an exquisitely worked light green gown with golden threads tracing the slit up its front - until the lower half of her thighs were exposed.

'Sit here, little slave,' she said pointing to the ground by her side. 'Tell me what you think of these young men. Are they to your taste?' Caristia sat on the cool flagstones and curled her feet under her bottom. 'What about that one, the one with the spear, the naked one. Does his muscular body fill you with desire? And look between his legs. Look at the nature of his manhood. How large it is; too big perhaps for you.' Arria Sulla stared at the young men, absently curling Caristia's hair between her fingers, then as if suddenly waking from a dream she pulled her hand away and sat up straight. 'Be quiet girl! Lucretius Fronto approaches.'

Fronto marched between the young men, nodding to some of them, joking and laughing with others. He was comfortable in their company and, because of his high rank, they were all keen to ally themselves to him, laughing readily at his quips and nodding seriously at his thoughtful observations. He greeted Arria Sulla by bowing and she held out her hand. He took it carefully, as if it was a prized treasure, lifted it to his lips and kissed it slowly.

'You look delightful, Arria Sulla. A delectable prize of womanhood amongst these sweating boys. I hope your accommodation is suitable?'

She nodded and started fiddling absently with Caristia's hair again.

'Yes, perfectly. Will you escort me amongst these young sportsmen?'

'Yes lady. I can see that the closeness of their bodies arouses you.'

'A little, perhaps,' she said haughtily. 'A little.'

He smiled and beckoned her forward. She took his arm and trailed her hand back to Caristia, motioning her to keep up.

'I have seen your young slave before. Indeed I would have taken her for myself if that rogue Rufo would have sold her to me.'

'I think she would have been wasted on you my lord. She has a keen instinct for pleasure.'

'I do not think wasted, madam,' he said unable to disguise his annoyance. 'Indeed, I wonder now if she would have been of the right quality at all. I would probably have had to let her go in the end anyway. I believe you have one of my cast-offs at the moment. Now what was her name? Yes, it comes back to me. Innocenti. I think I have it right. Innocenti.'

'Yes I do, my lord. Though I do not find her very satisfactory. She tires too quickly. She is more like a lady than a slave. Too delicate for her calling. Too fragile for a true slave of pleasure. I will return her if you wish. She may suit you more the second time around.' She laughed, grabbed Caristia's hand and pulled her up alongside. 'But not this one. She is too special to me.'

Arria Sulla stopped and kissed Caristia full on the mouth, pulling her close and tipping her head slightly back. As Caristia responded, extending her tongue into her mistress's mouth, Arria Sulla dropped her hand between Caristia's thighs and laid her fingers against her soft cunt. Caristia lifted herself up on the fingers, opening her legs enough to allow them to slip between the easily opened, wet flesh. Arria Sulla pulled back.

'See, my lord Fronto. See how the child abandons herself to the simplest pleasures.' Arria Sulla removed her hand. Caristia stood, panting slowly, licking her lips, expecting instructions, awaiting the demands of pleasure. 'I do not think you have anything to compete with one such as this. And if you did, I wager you would not risk testing her qualities against my own little slave of fire.' She laughed and pushed Caristia away.

Fronto frowned, for a moment unsure what to say. He pursed his lips.

'That is a challenge, madam. And one I will bear in mind.'

He led the way to a circular enclosure created by a barrier of timber hurdles, where two naked men with dumbbell-shaped leather gloves were engaged in a vicious boxing match. The shorter of the two, heavily muscled and brutish was getting the better of his opponent, holding his thumbs out and gouging at his enemy's already blooded and swollen eyes before finally delivering a heavy blow to the battered face, which knocked his victim unconscious to the ground. Arria Sulla smiled at the victor as he turned, panting and breathless from the effort. Sweat streamed down his well-defined muscles, running to his groin, soaking his genitals. He shone in the bright sunlight of the early afternoon like a glistening god.

Fronto and Arria Sulla stepped over the barrier, created from heavy timber hurdles, the crossbars of which were sturdy square pieces set in the upper wedge of the X-shaped supports.

'He is a fine specimen my lord Fronto,' said Arria Sulla as she poked at the boxer's stomach then rubbed her hands across his glistening chest. 'He is well muscled and firm and here,' she ran her hand down to his genitals, 'and here, he is well endowed but not, by the feel of him, excited even by the touch of a lady.'

'He has just won in combat, lady. He must be helped to recover.'

She threw her head back disdainfully.

'Caristia. Clean him with oil. He still smells of his combat. I would have him smelling sweetly.'

She motioned to her servants but Fronto interrupted her instructions.

'I will have my servant fetch oil and a basin. He will assist.'

Arria Sulla told Caristia to kneel by the boxer's side until she was needed. Caristia knelt obediently beside the sweating man and inhaled his aroma - the sweet smell of battle. Its harsh, salty tang excited her. It smelled like semen and she rocked forward slightly on her knees so that her face was as close as she dare put it to his flaccid genitals. She inhaled again, this time holding her breath and allowing the scent of his cock - his smooth-skinned venous cock that hung heavily in the parting between his weighty testicles - to penetrate her from within. Its aroma filled her with need and she rocked forward again, hoping she would not be seen as she abandoned caution for the sake of getting her face close enough to his cock to feel its radiant heat. The sound of Arria Sulla's voice became a distant echo as Caristia's eyes flickered upward and she was filled with a dizzy headiness.

A young man, dark-haired and handsome, ran up to the enclosure carrying a flask of oil and a shallow basin. He was naked except for a tightly-pulled cloth, drawn up between his legs and tied off around his slim waist. Fronto beckoned him to approach and he stepped athletically over the hurdle barrier.

'Master,' he said slightly out of breath.

'Drusus. I want you to help this slave clean up the boxer, oil him and make him sweet so that my lady can approach him without offence.'

Caristia looked up at the young man, her head still filled with the giddy scent of the boxer and her mind dazzled by the images that closeness to his body had conjured up in her. His elegant beauty distracted her from the animal attraction

50

of the massive boxer and the pictures that filled her mind were replaced with an image of youthful beauty. Drusus's full lips and steely blue eyes beguiled her and his tousled dark hair and short growth of beard made her mouth dry. He looked down at her and though he could not speak - it was more than his life was worth - somehow he managed to pass her a message of intimate complicity. It was as if their eyes passed mutual messages, as if speech was irrelevant, as if the rest of the world was untrained in their new method of communication.

Drusus knelt beside Caristia and handed her the basin. She stretched out her hands, imagining she was stretching them to encircle him, to wrap her arms around him and pull him down on top of her. She could tell he felt the same. He emptied the flask of oil into the basin. It ran from the spout in a gush, splashing into the shallow curve of the bowl and flowing up its edges before settling back into a dense pool of gold. He dipped a cloth into the bowl and scooped up some of the golden oil. She watched it drip as he reached out to the boxer's chest and rubbed the liquid into the bronzed, sweating skin. The sharp, slightly metallic scent of the oil mixed with the heady scent of the boxer and drifted down onto Caristia as if she had been lifted into a heavenly cloud. She trembled as she held out the bowl and bit her lips when Drusus again dipped the cloth into the shallow pool of fluid gold.

Remaining on her knees, Caristia rubbed the oil into the boxer's body, stretching up to reach his chest where Drusus had started and dropping her buttocks down onto the backs of her heels as she worked downwards. Some of the oil ran down her arms, into her armpits, onto her breasts then, urged on by her movements, down between her legs. All the time she watched Drusus and she knew that, whenever he had a chance, he also stole a glance at her. She rubbed the insides of the boxer's muscular thighs, reaching her oil-soaked hands around his testicles, embrocating them, feeling their weight, then circling her fingers around his cock, massaging it, pulling it, teasing it until, as she held it in her hands, she felt it thickening and extending.

The boxer's cock lengthened under her touch, its skin tightening over the throbbing veins and its glans swelling as she cradled it. She drew her face against it and let its pulsating beats heat her cheeks and she opened her mouth, still looking at Drusus and wishing it was him, as she prepared to take the now fully stiff cock between her open lips.

'Your little servant has done a fine job, lady. Indeed she has brought life about where her mistress failed.'

Arria Sulla's face darkened at the insult. For a moment she stared at Caristia, her slave, her belonging, holding the oiled cock near to her open mouth then, as if seized by a fit, she kicked out at the girl, knocking her over onto her side. Drusus stepped back as Arria Sulla kicked out again at Caristia, now bringing her legs up and folding her arms around her waist to protect herself.

'Still she gets the better of you, lady. See how easily she avoids your rightful punishment. It is almost as though this possession of yours is mistress herself.'

Arria Sulla pursed her lips, stamped her foot and screeched for her Nubians. They ran to her side as, unable to control herself, her face reddened.

'Take the girl!' she screamed. 'Take her and bind her so that she cannot avoid her punishment! Bind her!' The Nubians looked around, unsure what to do. 'Use anything!' screeched Arria Sulla. 'Just do as I order!' They dragged over one of the heavy hurdles from the barrier and set it down in the centre of the ring. 'Yes that. Bind her to that!' she ranted.

They lifted the cowering Caristia from the ground, turning her to face downwards before placing her lengthwise along the sharp upper edge of the crossbeam. She pulled herself away from it as her weight fell against its rim but one of the black slaves held her firmly with his hand and her wriggling only caused her more pain. The other Nubian ran to the side of the ring and undid some thin leather thongs that bound together one of the hurdles, dipped them in a water bowl to make them supple, then began securing Caristia to the hurdle. He bound her hands to the two front legs and her ankles to the other two, then while the other black slave kept the weight of his hand on her back, he bound her by the waist to the crossbeam. The weight of her body and the pressure of the tight bonds pulled her hard against the harsh edge of the timber beam. She hung her face to the side as it dug in between her breasts, down the centre of her stomach, then most painful of all, it ran between the open lips of her sex, nipping the tip of her clitoris before parting her outer labia wide.

She turned her head sideways and saw Drusus standing, holding the bowl of oil. He smiled at her, a secretive smile of alliance, and the idea of his sympathy filled her stomach with a thrill of nervous anxiety. A short piece of wood with cords at each end was pulled across her mouth and, as she bit down onto it, the cords were pulled tightly around the back of her head and knotted.

'Now bring something that will made her buttocks sting,' shouted Arria Sulla, still red-faced and angry. 'I want the impudent slave to suffer. I want her to beg for it to stop. There! Over there! Those sticks they are using to fight each other. Use one of those.'

The Nubians fetched two of the sticks and offered them for Arria Sulla's approval. She nodded insistently, wanting the punishment to get underway. Fronto took one of the sticks and held it up, knowing he could easily irritate Arria Sulla by delay.

'A fine cane,' he said, twisting it slowly between his fingers. 'Bamboo. Brought from the east in the land they call China. See how it flexes and yet, at the same time, it is strong enough to resist too much bending. Look at the raised knuckles along its length - hard and unyielding rings that strike the skin like a gouging thumb.'

He rested the tip on the ground and held the cane against his side, measuring its length before holding it up and whipping it through the air. It swished loudly, bending only slightly even though he slashed it down as fast as he could.

'Just get on with it,' insisted Arria Sulla as another of her Nubians brought her a chair to sit on. She opened the front of her skirt as she sat, exposing her dark, carefully trimmed pubic hair to the glint of the sun. 'Get on with it! I want to hear her scream!'

Fronto smiled, passed the cane back to the Nubian and turned to Arria Sulla.

'It will be interesting to see your little slave beg, though I do not know if she will be begging for her punishment to stop.'

He smirked and stood behind her chair.

The Nubians stood on each side of Caristia, each holding one of the bamboo canes diagonally across his chest. Arria Sulla nodded to one of them and he stood back and lifted the cane above his shoulder, twisting the tip high into the air before bringing it down swiftly onto Caristia's waiting bottom. She tightened herself as she heard it sweeping through the air. She brought her buttocks together and tensed herself, and the insides of her thighs dug into the sharp edges of the beam and the centre of her sex ached more as the harsh contact of the top edge against her clitoris increased. She saw Drusus looking down at her and again felt the tingling of anxious joy as she was aroused by his concern, then she tightened her eyes together in an involuntary wince as the swishing sound stopped and was replaced with a sudden smacking thud.

The cane struck both her buttocks across their centre. She was so exposed, tied across the beam of timber, that nothing hindered the contact; it was full, direct and excruciating. Her mouth opened as the breath was knocked from her and, in the instant it took for the pain to shoot throughout her whole body, bubbles of foaming saliva ran from her wide lips. The servant held the cane there for a moment, as if allowing it to regain its power, or to pass on any pain that was left in it, then when he lifted it away and the strip of skin it had struck was exposed to the air, the stinging pain increased. It was like fire, as if she was being branded, and she gulped for air.

She held her breath, keeping herself tight and listened again as the second blow came down. It was harder than the first, slightly lower and against even tenderer skin, and the angle it made against her caused her, in an involuntary reflex, to rear back. But there was no give in her bonds, nowhere to rear back to, and her action only pressed her more against the harsh edge of timber. Again she was saturated with pain but, as the cane lifted away and she waited for the next, her stomach filled with an expectation which, although tinged with the excitement of fear, was built from the delicious expectation of increased suffering.

She opened her eyes and looked at Drusus. He was still staring at her and his compassion, his loving sympathy, filled her with a novel, overwhelming sensation. She had never felt it before, but she knew what it was, and she allowed her whole self to soak into his eyes as the bamboo swept down for a third time. Again it found a different spot, a little lower still, almost at the faint crease between her bottom and the tops of her thighs. It stung even more deeply, mingling as it did with the previous blows, which were still reverberating along her nerves. She felt she could scream but now she knew it would only be for more, and she stared at Drusus and opened her mouth wide. Even though she felt it, this time it was not as an expression of pain but an expression of desire, a reciprocation of his own loving stare. She could do nothing more, she felt completely exposed to him and only hoped that with each subsequent blow, with each increase in her delectable suffering, he would see that all the desires within her were for him.

Each time the burning cane struck her bottom, each time it laid another red stripe across her tender skin, she strained against her unyielding bonds and the tension she created - contained inside her tortured body - fed her ever-growing passion. Each thump of the swishing stick, each smack of its knuckled length, drove her further into an ecstasy of pain, its ultimate end already declaring its power as it fought against the immovability of her body. The only change in her position was the contact her sex made with the edge of the diagonal bar. The swelling of her labia and the engorging of her clitoris pressed her flesh tighter against the beam, and the more the pressure and pain increased, the more her soft flesh swelled and the more her throbbing clitoris extended and crushed against the hard surface.

Arria Sulla told the black servant to step back so that the other one could take over. His blows were harder, more vicious, and he struck not only Caristia's thighs but her back and shoulders. Still she did not scream and, even though she blinked longer than normal, allowing the images in her mind to fill her completely, she kept her gaze on Drusus, showing him her wetness and the bliss of her pain. When the other Nubian was ordered to join in and they both rained a storm of alternate blows down on her agonized body, she felt her orgasm running through her, setting her on fire and consuming her with a blaze of ecstasy.

She watched Drusus all the time as her tightly secured body filled with bliss and the continuing blows caused the zenith of her final pleasure to persist at an unending peak.

'I think your little slave is gaining more from her punishment than she is learning, my lady,' said Fronto mockingly.

'Stop!' shouted Arria Sulla to her slaves. 'Stop the beating!' She looked around wildly for some other way of punishing her victim. She saw a heavy punch bag used by the boxers for training and ordered Caristia tied to it. The Nubians held the still jerking girl face forward against the leather bag, wrapped her arms around the top and secured them to the rope from which the bag hung. They drew her knees as far around the bag as they could, joining them with a length of rope before drawing her feet back and securing them on the opposite side of the heavy bag.

As soon as Caristia felt the smooth, sweat-shone leather against her splayed sex lips her orgasm started again. It was as though her body still had to bring it out, as though her joy had set in train something unstoppable. She gripped herself against the punch bag, pressing her wet face against the shiny leather and squeezing her open cunt flatly against the bulky bag to which she was secured. The smell of the leather filled her nostrils and again an aching grew deep within her groin. Arria Sulla ordered the Nubians to spank her with their bare hands and, as soon as the first smacking blow landed, her persisting orgasm surged through her in a fresh wave and drove her into an uncontrollable grasping spasm. It collected all the pent up desire that had been held back when she was tied to the timber beam and released it as though a dam had burst. As she pulled herself against the punch bag and released the wave of bliss she groaned loudly. The punch bag swung from side to side as the Nubians spanked her bottom. She tightened herself against it as much as her bonds would allow, rubbing her wet labia against the leather, pressing her hard clitoris fully against it, bending her knees and pulling up her ankles as though she was on the bare back of a galloping stallion. The spanking continued unabated, striking her sore bottom, smacking loudly with each blow and, all the time, her orgasm persisted, burning her like flames licking from an unquenchable fire of joy.

Fronto was still teasing the angry Arria Sulla when they took Caristia down. Still jerking with the remnant convulsions of her ecstasy she lay on the ground with her arms pulled up over her breasts and her legs bent so that her knees touched her elbows. Fronto's teasing turned to affection and he calmed Arria Sulla, stroking first her hair and forehead then, as her tension eased and she began to respond to his attention, running his hand between her legs and touching her sex. He ordered all the slaves to wait in the colonnaded area and Caristia was dragged roughly across the ground by the Nubians. They let her go as if they were delivering a sack and she slumped against one of the ribbed columns of the covered terrace.

She put her hands between her legs and felt her sex lips, the swollen flesh soft and silky and wet. She caressed with her fingers and their tips slid inside without any pressure. She felt the pulsating tip of her clitoris and as soon as she made contact with it, it started to beat and swell again. Drusus was standing by and she looked up at him. He was tall and his eyes shone like green crystals in the half-light beneath the covered colonnade. He looked back at her, but as soon as their eyes met he looked away, afraid they might be seen and afraid Caristia would be punished again. Caristia looked away too, not because of fear but in deference to her paramour.

She watched Fronto leading Arria Sulla into a wooden shelter used by athletes to store javelins. As a penance given them by their trainer because of their poor performance, a group of young men were scourging themselves with whips and Caristia could see that Arria Sulla could not take her eyes from them. Caristia's mistress leant against the side of the shelter, her elegant body bent slightly back as she watched the young men through a slit in the wall. Fronto pulled her arms back and draped them over a javelin he held parallel to the ground. She allowed him to bend her arms, not helping him but not resisting, and she opened her lips slightly as he bent her elbows over the javelin and pulled her hands back to her stomach where he tied them with cord. She dropped her head back a little but did not take her eyes from the naked young men. Fronto lifted her skirt and tucked the hem between the tightly held javelin and the dipping curve of the small of her back. Her smooth-skinned bottom was exposed to his view and he knelt behind it, running his hands across her smooth, rounded buttocks, then when he had stared at it enough, licking it slowly with his tongue.

Caristia could see the glint of his saliva on Arria Sulla's cheeks as Fronto trailed his tongue slowly across her skin. The sight of her mistress bound like a slave to the javelin, being licked by another of her class, filled Caristia with shivers of excitement. She looked at Drusus and her shivers of joy turned to a sudden shudder that caused her to shrug involuntarily and draw her shoulders up. She licked her lips, looking again at Arria Sulla who was now - although still fixated by the men as they punished themselves with the leather flails - tipping her bottom towards Fronto, opening her buttocks wider and encouraging his tongue to go between her voluptuous cheeks.

Caristia tasted the salt on her lips, and as she watched she found herself mimicking her mistress, bending against one of the columns, stretching her arms back as though bound to a javelin and sticking her bottom out in the hope that a man's tongue would lick along the valley between her buttocks. She looked at Drusus - only momentarily because she dared not look away from Arria Sulla for too long - but she could see he dared not move, he knew his master's temper and was too afraid. She caught the eye of one of the Nubians and he stepped towards her. She bent her arms back, showing him that she wanted to be tied like her mistress, and he picked up a long stick and wedged it into the crook of her elbows, pushing it between them and pressing it against her back. She felt the strain and pulled forward against it and, as she did, he took hold of her hands and offered her a shorter, thicker stick to hold on to. It had leather cords trailing from each end and they flicked against her face as she grabbed it. Straight away he bound her wrists and tied her to it, then pulling it back violently, he wedged it between her teeth and pulled the trailing thongs around her head. She choked as her mouth was suddenly and unexpectedly forced open, then filled. She flared her nostrils like a straining mare and gasped for air as Fronto, the palms of his hands on the insides of her mistress's thighs, opened Arria Sulla's buttocks and forced his tongue against the delightful darkness of her anus.

Caristia watched the tip of his tongue open the muscular ring, working its way in and driving Arria Sulla to tighten herself with a wave of stiffening rapture. The Nubian gripped the stave across Caristia's mouth and lifted her off the ground. She gasped through her nostrils and clenched her teeth tightly around the wooden bar. She hung in his hands, her feet kicking as she tried to twist herself so as not to lose sight of her mistress. The Nubian laughed and spun her back and forth. Caristia saw Arria Sulla in fleeting images as Fronto delved his tongue deep into her anus, opening it, making it receptive, making it wet. She saw him take it out and bend her forward against the strain of the javelin across her elbows and she watched, captivated, as he plunged his cock, suddenly and deeply, in one thrusting movement. Caristia could sense Arria Sulla's stifled a scream and, as she saw Fronto holding the javelin and riding her, plunging deeply, bringing himself to orgasm, the slave dropped her onto his own stiff cock. She felt the swollen glans between her legs and opened herself, not knowing whether he wanted her cunt or her anus. Then she felt it penetrate and her eyes widened and she clenched her teeth as tightly as she could, biting into the timber bar in her mouth, straining for breath through her nostrils. The huge cock filled her anus completely and when he thrust it further it expanded until it would hardly move.

Saliva flowed from Caristia's mouth, running over the bar between her teeth, tricking down her chin and dripping onto her naked breasts. She saw Fronto calling the young men over and watched as he bent Arria Sulla forward, curling her head down until her back was a delectable arch, so they could bring their whips down on her straining body. Each time a whip cracked against her back or smacked sharply against the upperpart of her buttocks, Caristia's anus dilated and allowed the Nubian's cock to go deeper. Each stinging blow on her mistress's naked skin caused Caristia to want filling even more, and as the blows rained down and Fronto tightened with his orgasm, Caristia took it all. Her clitoris throbbed as the Nubian forced her head down on the ground and bent her like her mistress. She did not know who beat her, she did not know who wielded the whips but she buried her face in the dust, slurping around the stave that was bound between her teeth as the Nubian's cock stiffened in a final pulse of energy, then filled her completely with a surge of hot semen. The whipping continued but it was the heat inside her rectum which brought on the convulsions of her own climax, and they continued until the last blow was delivered across her stinging, red-striped bottom.

Caristia was helped to her feet by one of the Nubians. She was not sure if it was the one who had penetrated her or not. She stood unsteadily, allowing her orgasm to dissipate, allowing the tension in her body to slacken. The stave was taken from her mouth and her teeth marks were clearly visible on its surface.

Drusus stood beside her, looking away from her but conscious of her presence, his hands by his sides. He took hold of her shaking hand and, pressing it tenderly, whispered only one word close to her ear. 'Escape,' he said softly, and her heart started beating so rapidly again it made her gasp.

Chapter 7
The House of the Gladiators

When Bec had been taken from Rufo's house by Magnus he had, under Rufo's orders, dragged her to the House of the Gladiators, on the north side of the town on the road to the Nola Gate. This was the centre of gladiator training for the whole region, and for much of the empire. Slaves were sent here by their masters for training by Sparton, himself an accomplished winner of many past contests and, since achieving his freedom, a rich and sort after trainer. Although most of the gladiators were men there were some women and occasionally Rufo had a promising candidate trained. If successful a female gladiator could achieve a very high price and Bec, beautiful and brimming with uncontrollable rage, was the most promising candidate he had seen for a long time.

Sparton had recognised her potential straightaway and since she had been there, under his cruel and demanding tutelage, she had become accomplished at many of the most sought after fighting skills. She wrestled and boxed strongly, fought with sticks - a favourite of the Romans, handled a sword and a lance like a soldier and was fearless when forced into cages with wild animals. She was considered superior to many of the men who, if ordered by her mentor, Sparton, she took on without any qualms. Those who watched were struck by fear as she straddled her vanquished foes, spitting and biting and screaming like a devil from hell. Rufo visited the training camp every week, paying Sparton his fees and checking on the progress of his protégé. Each time he saw her, poised like a warrior, glinting in polished training armour or stripped naked, her muscular legs and arms oiled and flexing under the tension of sword, shield or spear, he grew more excited by the prospect of her value. Sparton said she was still difficult to handle but Rufo knew it was that very sense of uncertainty which would excite the crowd and make her command the highest price.

'She is like the great Theogenes, who fights his adversaries with such courage the crowd treats him as an emperor,' he told Rufo, pointing to a massive gladiator pinning his wrestling opponent to the ground. 'What an ox, eh Rufo? See him grasp the waist belt of his opponent, see how his leg tackle brings his enemy quickly to the ground as if he was a sack of flour. Only last week he lost his teeth in the arena, but swallowed them instead of spitting them out so his adversary could not know his injury. Theogenes! Present yourself to Olconio Rufo.'

Theogenes ran over in short, paced steps and stood before them. He was naked except for a silver-linked chain around his muscular waist.

'He is magnificent,' said Rufo, looking at the perfectly proportioned gladiator from all angles. 'Wonderful! May I?'

'Of course. Of course,' said Sparton keenly. 'See what a prize he is. Go on. Check him. You will find no fault. '

Rufo looked closely at Theogenes, then staring into his eyes Rufo cradled his genitals in his hand. He weighed them, nodding with satisfaction as the gladiator stood completely still. He encircled the naked man's thick cock with his fingers and nodded with satisfaction at its fleshy girth.

'And what of my student?' he said turning away. 'Is she coming on well?'

'Bring out our black-haired tigress!' shouted Sparton. 'Bring out the warrior Bec.'

A heavy gate clanked and two men with spears entered a dark tunnel. There was a brief pause then, in a cloud of dust and spitting with anger, Bec was driven into the arena. The gladiators gathered around edged forward excitedly and shouted encouragement to the wild-eyed tigress. She bent her legs wide and crouched, turning to the right and left, baring her teeth and snarling. She was a wild animal, clad in only a black leather thong pulled tightly between her legs, her body glistening with sweat in the hot sun. Her firm breasts rose to hard peaks at her nipples and, when she tensed her thighs, the outline of her cunt was impressed against the inside of the tight leather moulded against it.

'You have bred a fine animal, Sparton,' gloated Rufo as he gazed at his prize possession. 'She looks indomitable.' He smiled as a thought occurred to him. 'How would she fair against your favourite, I wonder?'

Sparton beckoned Theogenes to him.

'My dear Theogenes, let us see your skills against this spitting animal. See if you can tame her, bring her to heel. But mind, she must not be injured or Rufo here will be charging me!'

Theogenes looked hard at Bec. He bent his legs slightly, curling his toes into the dusty ground, breathing deeply as he opened his hands, holding them forward, bending the tips of his fingers, enticing her to approach him. Bec turned to him and bent, reaching forward in readiness and squatting as low as she could so that she was perfectly balanced. The thin leather gusset of her thong pulled tightly against the flesh of her cunt, dipping into the central valley and pulling against the moist inner leaves. She licked her fleshy lips, then with no warning she lurched forward and grabbed Theogenes by the throat.

She had taken him by surprise with her sudden rush, had broken behind his guard and thrown him off balance. She pressed her thumbs against the front of his throat and stared into his reddening face. She spat into his eyes, then following up the confusion she had caused in his mind, stepped past him on his right side, swept her right leg backwards, knocked both his legs from beneath him and sent him crashing to the ground. She released her grip on his throat as he fell in a cloud of red dust. For a moment she stood astride him, throwing her head back, shrieking loudly as if the victory had been won - but her triumph was short-lived. Theogenes turned quickly, grabbed her right ankle and punched hard behind her knee. She crumpled as her leg gave way and as she lost her balance he reached high up her right thigh, encircled it with his muscular arm and brought her down.

Caught off guard she landed heavily, her shoulder and face striking the dusty ground before she had time to bring her hands up to save herself. She spat mud from her mouth as Theogenes linked his arm behind her elbows and squeezed them together behind her back. He strained her backwards, lifting first her face from the ground then her shoulders until her firm breasts were exposed. She squirmed like a serpent but could not escape; Theogenes had her fast and was not going to let her go.

'Your little tigress is not in the first class yet, my dear Rufo. She must learn much before she would be the match of Theogenes.'

The gladiators surrounding the pair laughed and clapped in mock applause. Bec's black eyes shone with the reflection of their taunting faces and her mind filled with uncontrollable anger. She relaxed and dropped forward in Theogenes's grip. He relaxed his hold and the instant she felt it easing she raised her back against the lock and broke free. She turned on him and sank her teeth into his shoulder. Blood poured from the wound and when she looked up it dripped from her lips and stained her teeth. Theogenes looked surprised. Taken unawares he was unsure what to do. He looked across to Sparton, hoping he would unleash him; allow him free reign over this upstart animal.

'Do not injure her Theogenes! Do not injure her!' shouted Sparton with some anxiety. 'But do not allow her to humble you. The time of your retirement is not yet come. Show us that you are still the most skilled gladiator in the whole of Rome.'

As if released from binding chains Theogenes brushed Bec aside with a single blow. She fell to the ground and growled at him like an injured dog. He dropped astride her and pinned her shoulders down with his knees. She tossed her head from side to side and he took her face in his hand, pinching her cheeks until she stopped.

'Do not injure her!' shouted Rufo nervously. 'Do not injure my investment!'

Theogenes lifted his naked buttocks from Bec, reached back and took hold of the top edge of her leather thong. He pulled it up, pinching the flesh of her sex between the narrow gusset and the tops of her thighs. He twisted it until he saw a glimmer of pain on his victim's face. She had revealed her weakness, her submission to his strength, even if only for a fraction of a second and he ripped the thong upwards, tearing the leather laces that held it on her hips and exposed her cunt to the searing air. He held the thong up like a trophy and the jeering group around them closed in and shouted loudly.

'My investment!' shouted Rufo anxiously, trying in vain to see what was going on behind the closed ranks of the gladiators. 'My investment!'

Theogenes pressed his knees down on Bec's shoulders, raising himself up so that his full weight pinned her down. His cock dangled above her face and he let its tip brush her lips. Still holding the thong in the air he reached back again and ran his fingers through her dark pubic hair and her sex lips. Their fleshiness opened under his touch and his fingers slipped easily inside. Bec tightened her expression and licked out with her tongue, tantalizing Theogenes to let his cock come closer to her mouth. He laughed, and at the same time as he drove his fingers into her sex, he squeezed the leather thong into a ball and stuffed it into her mouth. She fought against him but he was too powerful. One of the gladiators handed him a wide leather belt and he wrapped it across her mouth, sealing the thong inside, then tightened it and buckled it behind her head.

Bec twisted and turned as she lay pinned between Theogenes's legs. He lowered himself and rubbed his cock against her cheeks, encouraging it to harden in his hand. She turned her face away but he held her long black hair and pulled her back into position. The gladiators cheered him on as he sprang to his feet, grabbed Bec's wrists and spun her around. She fell forward as he took the spare end of the belt around her head, yanked her wrists up between her shoulder blades and bound them tightly together. He dragged her across the dusty arena, the crowd of shouting men milling around excitedly. Theogenes bent Bec forward, pulled down a rope that was hanging from a beam and secured her wrists to it. She hung on the rope, unable to keep her balance, suspended by her wrists.

Theogenes turned to Sparton and Sparton nodded approvingly.

'Yes Theogenes,' he called, 'punish your vanquished foe. Here, try her first with the cane.'

Sparton handed Theogenes a thin willow cane, as long as a man's arm and whisker thin. Sparton took it in his left hand and swished it by the side of his ear, testing its meagre resistance and listening to the sound as it cut through the thick air. He smacked it across the palm of his hand and rubbed the line it left with his thumb. He turned back to his victim, his cock now fully erect and throbbing. He rubbed his right hand across Bec's muscular buttocks. She twisted away from his touch and he smacked her bottom as if telling her to stay still. The loud smack only caused her to twist more and she kicked backwards, catching him on the shin before he smacked her again, even harder.

He faced away from her and pressed his hips against hers, then with the cane in his left hand he encircled her wriggling waist and clasped his forearm beneath her stomach. He lifted her slightly off the ground and the feeling of his power, and her enforced subjugation to it, caused her to kick even more frantically. He tilted to his right and lifted her onto his hip. Again he used his right hand to smooth the skin of her bottom. Again she began thrashing wildly and again he smacked her hard. The gladiators let out a shout as the spanking sound filled the small training arena, and when Theogenes brought his hand down again and a redness started to appear across Bec's bottom, they shouted even louder.

Their roaring cries filled his ears. It was as though he was in the arena again, pandering to the crowd as they encouraged him to humiliate his enemy. He smacked Bec again. She hung against his hip for a moment, absorbing the pain, suffering its penetration, before starting to fight against him with renewed vigour. Another smack, again slapping loudly as the flat palm contacted her tensed flesh. The gladiators started to chant rhythmically and Theogenes timed his smacks to the syllables of their dirge - *'Fla-gell-o! Fla-gell-o!'*. Each time they started he drew his hand back and, after holding it above his head while they sang out a long expectant *'gell'*, he swept it down so that the smacking sound coincided with their loud crescendo *'O!'*. Again and again Theogenes spanked her writhing bottom, again and again she twisted and turned in vain attempts to escape his grasp and again and again the gladiators roared their approval as they joined in with their chorus.

Bec's bottom reddened - two patches across her pale skin slightly bigger than Theogenes's hand - and as she tired she slumped more heavily on the rope, allowing her buttocks to open so that her sex was easily visible between them. It glistened with moisture and, as she opened herself more with each blow, the soft mounds of flesh that surrounded the wet slit engorged and opened. Theogenes tightened his grip around her waist and lifted her higher, bending his face down to her bottom then licking the reddened patches caused by the spanking. She kicked her feet but one of the other gladiators took hold of them and restrained her. Theogenes opened her buttocks and let his tongue slip along her exposed crack. The soft edges opened under the touch and he probed the base of her clitoris, encouraging it to swell before letting his tongue delve deeply into the dark, moist interior of her cunt.

He licked her deeply, forcing open her reddened buttocks so he could push his face fully between them. He slid his left hand, still with the thin cane in its grasp, up between her legs and held onto her pubic hair, pulling it and stretching the flesh of her cunt so that it tightened against his tongue. When he pulled his face away her sex was fully dilated and soaked. He released his grip on her and she slumped heavily on the rope, a gasp stifled by the gag in her mouth exploding from her nostrils with a heavy snort. Two gladiators immediately took hold of her ankles and splayed them wide. Theogenes stood between her open buttocks, smacking her rhythmically as he brought the tip of his throbbing cock closer to her vulnerable, wet cunt. When its tip touched the soft outer leaves she struggled hard, throwing her head back and twisting her shoulders, but it was impossible to escape; she was completely trapped.

Theogenes pushed his cock in deep and, bending forward and reaching beneath her, he lashed the cane repeatedly across her breasts, striping them red and hardening her nipples as he drove himself to a massive and convulsing orgasm. He kept up the thrashing while he finished, embedding his cock each time another rush of semen spurted from him, and only when he finally stood back and took a deep breath did he drop the cane and let Bec hang, gasping noisily through her nostrils on the rope that held her wrists.

Suddenly there was a stir at the rear of the training yard. Arria Sulla's Nubians were making way for their mistress. Caristia walked behind her, dressed only in a short tunic and looking down shamefully, still suffering daily beatings for her conduct at the gymnasium and constantly threatened with more punishment by her hard-to-please mistress.

'Caristia! Here! Closer!' Arria Sulla shouted angrily. 'Do I have to have you spanked just because you are too slow? Here!'

Arria Sulla swung around and slapped Caristia on the side of the face. Caristia flinched with the stinging pain and, as her cheek reddened she dropped her head and hurried close to her mistress's side.

Sparton saw the entrance of the important visitor, and rushed over to the gladiators gathered around Bec and Theogenes. Caristia looked up enough to see him kicking at them and, more afraid of him than eager to satisfy their lust, they backed away. Theogenes was the last to move, but with a dark scowl that foretold his continuing intentions he stood aside. Caristia gasped at the sight of the mostly naked gladiators and of the especially beautiful Theogenes.

Sparton quickly unbuckled the belt from around Bec's head and she spat out the leather thong plugging her mouth. She gasped loudly, then as the rope around her wrists was untied she fell back sweating and panting, her legs apart and her sex lips glistening with Theogenes's semen. She wiped a hand between her legs and, glaring hard at Theogenes, she licked the wetness from her fingers. Her face was covered in dust, sticking to the saliva that had forced its way past the gag and caked her high-boned cheeks. She smeared the semen over her lips then licked it away and swallowed it slowly. With her mouth open she glared around her like an animal looking for a victim.

Rufo stiffened, and when he saw Caristia he pursed his lips, still smarting from the compromise of having to sell her to Arria Sulla.

'Madam,' he said, wringing his hands and approaching her. 'You grace us with your presence. Have you come to see the entertainment? Perhaps Sparton should not have been so quick to bring it to a close.'

'Perhaps,' she mused. 'Yes, perhaps.'

'I can have them continue if that is your pleasure.' She looked back at Caristia and pursed her lips. Caristia dropped her eyes quickly.

Suddenly Bec sat up as she saw Caristia. Her eyes opened wide and she leapt to her feet and charged forward. Sparton only just managed to prevent her from getting at her prey and, as she kicked out wildly in his grasp, Arria Sulla dropped back in fear.

'Do not worry madam,' said Sparton reassuringly, as he handed Bec over to the strong arms of several gladiators. 'Our fiery tigress is not threatening you. It is your little servant that seems to be inflaming her. Perhaps she is jealous of her skills as a warrior! Perhaps she thinks she would be more successful with the beautiful Theogenes.'

He laughed as Arria Sulla stepped forward again and composed herself.

'My little servant has misbehaved much lately and a bout with your warrior, Theogenes, might serve as a useful lesson to her.'

'You joke of course madam!'

'No sir. I do not joke. Put her in the ring and let us witness her punishment.'

Sparton was unsettled, but aware of Arria Sulla's position and reputation he instructed Theogenes and armed him with a fine metal net.

'If it is punishment you want to see, madam, then Theogenes is more than able to provide it. Bring your servant forward. Let me see her potential as a gladiator!'

He laughed as Caristia was brought to him by the Nubians. She hung her head, unwilling to look towards Bec and frightened by what might happen if she met the eyes of any of the gladiators. The air smelled of sweat and dust and she felt it burning her throat as she gasped with fear. The Nubians released her arms and she stood shaking before Sparton. Suddenly a shudder came over her as if she was caught by a cold draft and her face reddened with embarrassment. Rufo stood near Arria Sulla, trying hard to suppress the sense of injustice that burned inside him every time he looked at Caristia's pale beauty and innocent fragility.

'Will you not look up little slave?' asked Sparton as he held his hand beneath Caristia's chin. 'Surely you are not afraid of Sparton!' She glanced around as he lifted her face and from the corner of her eye she saw Bec having to be restrained by three of the gladiators. Caristia bit her lip anxiously as Sparton turned to Arria Sulla. 'I can see why you are having problems, madam. Your little slave has no voice. But I think I can help her find one.'

He told all the gladiators except Theogenes to back away and form a circle. The three holding Bec struggled to get her to move as she strained her legs out straight and dug her heels into the dusty ground. They tried to gag her but she bit one of them on the wrist and they gave up. In the end they bound her wrists and ankles with rope and dragged her face down to the edge of the small arena.

Spartan lifted Caristia in his arms and carried her into the arena. As he cradled her she felt like an offering, as though being offered as a sacrifice. He put her down in the centre and presented her ceremoniously with a short wooden sword. The gladiators laughed as she looked at it, unsure what to do. Sparton pressed it on her and she grasped it hopelessly.

Theogenes sprang forward, the silver chain at his waist shining in the bright sunlight. Caristia backed away as he approached, his naked flesh glistening with sweat and oil and his muscles flexing with every tiny movement of his athletic body. He twirled the net in a long low circle and its outer edges almost touched her ankles. She skipped back and tripped, falling on her back and dropping the wooden sword. The fall winded her and she gulped for air as her short tunic rode up and exposed the tops of her thighs and the smooth flesh of her freshly-shaved sex. The gladiators laughed at her embarrassment as she pulled the tunic down, then as she took up the sword again and regained her feet they clapped in mock applause.

Theogenes swirled the net again and this time it tangled around her right ankle. She tried to pull free but it was hopeless and her leg was lifted as he pulled her forward like a captured fish. She hopped, still holding the sword, her head filled with the jeering shouts of the surrounding gladiators, her body with the tingling hollowness of fear.

'Still I have not heard her speak, Theogenes. Her mistress is impatient for her words,' shouted Spartan. 'Give her a voice! Let us hear her!'

Theogenes pulled Caristia forward, her leg held up, fighting to keep her balance. She felt his savagery and was filled with fear but she also felt his strength and grew hot with desire. She tried to unravel the net from her foot, but as she bent down and reached forward he threw the net over her and tightened it. It covered her completely and as he drew it up it tightened around her, securing her, stopping her from moving, then as he gave it a sudden heavy tug it brought her down bodily to the dusty ground.

He dragged her around the arena and she rolled over in an uncontrolled bundle inside the ever-tightening net. She choked as the dust filled her mouth and her eyes stung with the dry dirt that was flung up. She felt exposed and humiliated but was powerless to do anything, powerless to escape and powerless to avoid her disgrace. He pulled her to him and lifted her high in the air, laughing at the sight of her, trapped inside the net, a tragic captive, squeezed firmly inside its mesh, unable to move. He carried her over to where Bec was still being held and nodded to her captors. They took the ropes from her wrists and ankles and lifted her to her feet, one of them holding each ankle and another two holding each arm. She writhed against them but even her anger could not bring about the strength to break free.

She spat at Caristia as Theogenes brought her closer. Her hatred for Caristia, borne from a sense of personal injustice, had now grown into an overpowering darkness of malice. Caristia wanted to turn away but she was held fast by the net. Theogenes brought them together, Bec spitting and struggling and Caristia, bound tightly in the net, the focus of Bec's animosity.

'We have still not heard her voice, Theogenes!' shouted Sparton. 'I hope you are not failing me!'

Theogenes fetched some rope and began tying Bec and Caristia together. Caristia felt the heat not only of Bec's struggling body, but of her hatred. It was like being licked by flames. As they were squeezed together her legs were pushed apart and she was made to fully face her adversary. She felt Bec's nipples pressing between the gauze of the mesh and touching her own. She felt their throbbing and their heat, and as the rope was tightened even more she felt the roughness of Bec's pubic hairs pressed against her own tender, freshly-shaved flesh. It made her shiver and, even in this fearful proximity to her enemy, she felt a wave of desire spread through her. Bec spat at her but still the desire was spreading within her.

She felt the mesh of the net being parted at the back and suddenly she could move slightly, just her buttocks. Her tunic was ripped upwards and her bottom exposed, then just as she was easing herself a little she tensed against Theogenes's smacking hand. She gasped as it struck. Bec glared at her, only inches away. Another smack and she tightened again, the pain intense, burning, penetrating, and her whole body lifted away from the source of the suffering. Because she was so constricted inside the net any movement pulled it tighter and any hope of getting away from the spanking was fruitless. Another even harder blow fell and her gasp turned into a grunt, then another, and this time the pain was so intense she cried out.

'At last! She speaks!' shouted Sparton. 'More, Theogenes! More!'

Bec wriggled against her captors and managed to drop slightly so that her face was against one of Caristia's nipples. She took it in her mouth and, just as another smack resounded against Caristia's bottom, bit it hard. Caristia screamed as the two pains came together, the burn from Theogenes's hand and the penetrating fire that ran from her nipples throughout her whole constricted body. She screamed again, and as she heard the shrieking tone of her own pain she felt a growing heat between her thighs. She screamed again and tightened her buttocks just enough to sense the wetness of her increasing excitement against the tightly pressed flesh of her cunt. She breathed in deeply and the expansion of her chest forced her erect nipple towards Bec, who bit harder, and when another smack arrived Caristia screeched in a high-pitched cry.

The net was parted a little further and she felt hands forcing her buttocks apart. The wetness from her cunt met the hot air and a wave of realisation of her predicament, her proximity to her enemy, exposure and the fierce beating sent a shiver through her. She felt her slit swelling, engorging, and as her buttocks were prised wider and she felt the heat of the first cock against her throbbing labia, the excitement within her flowed like water from a bursting dam. She screeched again, but this time not in pain, not in fear, but in an outburst of satisfaction as her first orgasm set fire to her nerves and scorched each part of her inner being.

She rode each cock as it was brought to her, not seeing any of them, only feeling their heat, their raised veins and their culminating bursts of semen. She sucked it up each time one finished inside her, drawing it in with the convulsions of her own orgasm, draining it until it was empty and she was ready for the next. Only then, when there was a slight pause before the next, did Bec's grip on her nipple relax, just for a moment so that she could catch breath and, as the next sank in and she groaned as it filled her, Bec bore down on her nipple again, clamping her teeth around it and biting as hard as she could.

Even after each of the gladiators had taken their turn Caristia moaned for more. She tilted her buttocks back as much as she could within the confines of the net, and inhaled deeply so that her nipple reached as far as possible into Bec's mouth. Sparton ordered Theogenes to release her, and when untangled she rolled onto her back and opened her legs wide. Semen dribbled down the insides of her thighs and the soft pinkness of her sex lips glistened with moisture in the sunlight. Her face was wet with sweat, her blonde hair in tangles and stuck to her face, and her lips swollen and slightly apart as she panted and gasped for air. Arria Sulla marched up to her, kicked her and told her to get up. Caristia stood, still shaking with the remnants of her orgasms. Her left nipple was reddened and stiff and her cheeks flushed when she saw her mistress staring at it.

'You are quite a little gladiator, Caristia,' said Arria Sulla, looking away thoughtfully. 'Perhaps I have mistaken your vocation,' she mused, turning over an idea in her mind.

Chapter 8
The Amphitheatre

The Amphitheatre at Pompeii, now in its one hundred and sixtieth year, lacked the grandeur and sophisticated planning of the gigantic Colosseum in Rome, but was nevertheless host to some of the best gladiators found in the Empire. Its high, open seating lent a bright and airy sense to its architecture and the roars of the crowd rose in waves from its stepped seating as fighters were tested in front of Pompeii's discerning clients. Some would find favour and perhaps be bought for combat in the capital, or perhaps Capua or Puteoli. Some were defeated then tortured and killed before the chanting crowd or perhaps, if only wounded in combat, their lives were offered up to the mercy of the graceless mob who stamped and jeered if the show was not to their liking. The gladiators entered the Amphitheatre by one of the two main external staircases which led to the outside of the upper tiers. From here they descended into the arena, sometimes to a fanfare of trumpets, sometimes heralded by a group of girls carrying banners or throwing flowers, but always to the shrieking adulation of the adoring yet capricious crowd.

Arria Sulla and her attendants entered by a small staircase at the head of the oval arena. Two flimsily clad girls escorted them to their seats. The crowd roared as pretty young girls, all naked except for green garlands in their hair, entered the arena throwing flowers with graceful circling of their slender arms. The petals rose in the hot air and some fluttered onto Caristia's face as she attended her mistress, already settling herself into a garland-decked box near the front.

Innocenti, only brought out by Arria Sulla because her mistress thought she looked pale, was made to stand by her mistress's side with her arms straight and her hands open and flat against the sides of her thighs. She bit her lips childishly as she swallowed in the heat of the sun, but when she looked down at her feet to avoid the glare, Arria Sulla swung around and smacked her hard across her scarcely covered buttocks. Innocenti shuddered and slapped her hands rigidly against her sides, staring straight ahead and barely able to stop her mouth quivering with the tremor of rising tears.

'Still, I said girl! Still!' shouted Arria Sulla.

Tears welled up in Innocenti's eyes. She looked pale and pitiful and Caristia felt a surge of concern as Arria Sulla, still dissatisfied with the girl's posture, swung at her again and smacked her. Innocenti broke into tears and the ill-tempered Arria Sulla grabbed the girl's tunic, lifted it up above her pert bottom and spanked her hard across both cheeks. Innocenti squirmed her hips out of the way, pushing the left one forward slightly as the stinging blow caused her to tense her buttocks tightly together.

'Stop crying girl!' shouted Arria Sulla. 'You test my patience!'

'Having problems with your slavegirls?' asked a familiar voice.

Arria Sulla swung around and glared at Fronto.

'Nothing I cannot cope with,' she retorted curtly.

'So I see,' he said, smirking.

'Stand still girl!' screeched Arria Sulla, and the weeping Innocenti pushed her arms back against her sides and flattened her hands on her hips. Her tunic did not drop down and her reddened buttocks remained exposed to any curious eyes

67

that looked at the humiliated girl.

Fronto stared briefly at Caristia and she dropped her eyes.

'Ah, the entertainment!' announced Fronto, turning around and gazing up at the tiered arena.

Two gladiators appeared at the top of one of the flights of stairs. The first one wore a bronze helmet with a broad flange at the neck pierced with two holes to fasten down the visor. The visor was riveted together and strengthened by a strip of bronze running from the brow to the chin. Hinged to the helmet behind the ears, a broader flange around the base of the helmet itself protected his thick neck and part of his massive, exposed shoulders.

The helmet of the second had a broad flange rising up over the brow then running round to protect the neck. This one's face was completely covered by two half visors formed from a network of bronze rings, attached at the sides and provided with tags which slotted into two bands on the cheek-guards below. The high crest ended in a griffin's head, and on either side of the helmet were sockets holding bright plumes. Over the forehead was a large Medusa head in relief. Neither of the men wore anything else, their muscular frames - shaved, oiled and burnished by slaves trained specifically for the purpose - were completely naked. The one with the plumed helmet had a long, heavy cock hanging down in front of large, weighty balls. The other had his cock tied by the stretched foreskin to a thin string that circled his waist. The tension of the string pulled his scrotum up and squeezed his balls outwards in two broad mounds.

Naked girls ran from behind them, strewing flowers as they danced in procession to the tops of the steps. The crowd turned and saw them and, as the two magnificent men marched down the steps into the arena, the crowd screeched with an outburst of unbridled pleasure and expectation. They jumped to their feet and cheered. Women opened the fronts of their tunics and exposed their breasts. Some lifted their skirts and showed their wet cunts, shouting to their heroes in the hope they would glance their way. Some women already waited near the exit, their hands between their legs and their fingers slipping between their fleshy slits as they imagined being chosen by the victor as he returned from doing battle. These women looked out from the dark tunnel towards the light of the arena, already picturing themselves thrown down by the savage victor and ridden viciously like a suffering animal. They saw themselves on their knees, their heads pulled back by their hair, screaming for it to stop only to have their faces forced into the dusty ground and held there until they were filled with the hot semen of their uncaring champion.

The two gladiators marched behind the girls. A woman threw herself at the one with the plumed helmet, took his cock in her mouth and began to suck it. Another tried to pull her away, eager herself to feel the massive glans on her tongue and its heat in her mouth. The gladiator brushed them both aside as if they were leaves and both of them fell immediately on two men in the crowd, sucking their cocks in a frenzy as the image of the mighty gladiator filled both their minds. Caristia brushed some of the flower petals from her face as the gladiators pounded up behind them. She smelled their muscular bodies and deep inside she felt the same yearning as all the other women that filled the uproarious arena. She stepped out slightly, looking towards Arria Sulla to make sure she was not noticed, and when the plumed gladiator passed she brushed herself against him as if inadvertently. She felt her nipples hardening, and as she felt them pressing against her thin tunic and she saw how close the bound cock of the gladiator was to her she felt the wetness running from the swelling flesh of her hot, aching vagina.

She watched Fronto behind Arria Sulla as she stood up excitedly at the edge of the box the moment the two gladiators engaged in combat. Each time they crashed together Fronto lifted Arria Sulla's skirt a little higher. Each time the crowd roared its approval Arria Sulla pressed her bottom back towards Fronto's rigid cock. When he had lifted her skirt enough to expose her bottom fully, Caristia felt her own eagerness overcoming her and stretched her hand back to a man behind her - an unseen stranger - inviting him to copy Fronto and showing him that, if he did, she would imitate her mistress.

Arria Sulla bent forward and Caristia stared at the point where the dark cleft between her buttocks opened to accommodate the swelling flesh that rose in semi-circular mounds on either side of the moist centre of her cunt. She saw the pinkness at its centre glisten as the satiny inner leaves were exposed to the light of the burning sun and, as the wet surfaces glinted, she felt her own cunt exposed between her legs as she too bent forward and the hem of her tunic was lifted to her waist.

She saw Fronto running a hand between Arria Sulla's legs, letting the full width of his palm force her thighs wide, allowing her sex to open and spread against his hand. Arria Sulla lifted her bottom and Caristia saw the darkness of her anus as, rolling her eyes upwards and moaning, Arria Sulla lifted herself as high as she could. The man behind Caristia spread his hand between her legs and she emulated her mistress, allowing his palm to press against her flesh, to open it and squash it and, as she eased down against the pressure she lifted her bottom upon it, allowing her buttocks to open until she felt the air against her sensitive anus.

The swords of the gladiators clashed loudly and an excited roar went up from the crowd. Arria Sulla let out a sharp scream as Fronto wrapped his left arm around her hips, lifted her up and smacked her bottom. The pale skin reddened immediately and Caristia urged her own bottom higher, inviting the man behind her to do the same as Fronto. Then, as one of the gladiators fell to the ground and a low groan of dismay erupted from the crowd, Caristia felt the man's arm encircling her hips and lifting her. Fronto delivered another smack, a loud spank with the full of his hand, and Arria Sulla twisted beneath it. She gasped and bit her lip as she prepared herself for the next. The crowd shouted as the fallen gladiator struggled to his feet and Caristia felt the breath knocked from her as, at last, she felt the stinging contact of the man's hand across her own upturned buttocks. She watched Arria Sulla's buttocks reddening as she wriggled beneath her beating, and Caristia imagined her own bottom to be the same, reddening and burning with each sharp spank. She cried out, louder and louder, trying to hear herself above the roaring crowd, and she felt her cunt, exposed as much as possible, melting with moisture as she burned with the pleasure of the spanking.

Fronto pushed his hand between Arria Sulla's shoulders and forced her head down. Her hair loosened from its silver clips and her ringlets fell in tangles around her face. He lifted his short tunic and took his cock in his hand. It was long and hard and Caristia saw the glans, deep red and throbbing, still swelling as he squeezed the venous shaft. She licked out her tongue, she wanted to suck it, to feel its heat, to taste its saltiness but, even as she reached forward he pushed it into the warm flesh of Arria Sulla's vagina.

Caristia turned, she wanted the same, she still wanted thrashing, she'd not had enough, but now she wanted to be filled as well. Her scorching bottom was insufficient to gratify her; now she wanted to be set on fire from deep within her body. A hand slapped her between the shoulder blades, knocking her forward and making her choke for breath. The smacking continued, harder and harder and, as she watched her mistress throwing her head up in ecstasy as Fronto drove harder and faster inside her, she pined for the same. Fronto grabbed Arria Sulla's hair and wrenched her head back. In a seizure of pleasure he stiffened, levelled his hips against her reddened buttocks and finished deeply inside her. There was a pause, as if the whole stadium had become silent, then Arria Sulla let out a piercing howl of delight, like a wolf calling in the night, then just as her head began spinning from lack of air, she snatched a rapid breath and started wailing again.

Caristia's ears filled with her mistress's yells, then suddenly she felt a heat against her anus, pressing at it, forcing it open. She gasped as it pushed harder, then with a suddenness that made her eyes widen, the pulsing cock entered the muscular ring and swelled tightly against the sensitive inner flesh. She gasped as it sank further, driving mercilessly into her rectum, filling her, setting her on fire, threatening to burn her alive. The smacking stopped but she barely noticed. She reached back; she wanted to feel the shaft before it disappeared completely inside her. She wanted to feel its thickness, the raised veins, its heat. But she was not allowed, it was inside her too fast, and as she screeched with the pain of penetration, her wrists were grabbed and brought together in the small of her back.

Something was wrapped around them, she did not know what, but as it tightened it brought her elbows together and drew her shoulders back. She kept her bottom held up, still inviting the cock, but her head dropped forward and her erect nipples scraped harshly against the back of a stone bench. Another thrust and the cock inside her rectum was buried to the hilt. She felt weighty balls pressing against her labia, opening and massaging. Her whole body was on fire, inflamed by the heat of the cock within her rectum. She was burning with the violation and she tried to look back but now it was impossible; she could hardly move. Her breasts were pressed hard against the back of the stone bench and her wrists were held so tightly against the middle of her back that it was impossible to get upright. She was helpless, overcome.

The thrusting continued, her buttocks wide open, the ring of her anus burning as the shaft of the hard cock ran inside it and the sensitive innards of her rectum tightening involuntarily like satin around the bulging cock. She saw Fronto pulling away from her mistress and a wave of anxiety filled her as she realised her misbehaviour. She tried to get away, squirming frantically, but it was pointless, she was a victim, unable to do anything other than another's will. She started screaming, both in pleasure and panic, then the man grabbed her hips, squeezed them and, with a final thrust and a massive deluge the cock finished inside her. It lurched as it filled her rear passage with repeated pulses of hot semen, each throb widening the shaft and tightening it almost unbearably against the dilated muscular ring of her anus. She hung on the pulsating cock, not daring to move, unable to breathe, unable to feel anything except overwhelming pleasure. Finally, when every drop had entered her, when she was soaked with it, the pressure subsided. She was pushed forward and her head dropped over the back of the stone bench. The bonds around her wrists were slackened then fell away and she slid sideways and fell to the floor with semen dribbling freely from her anus. She gasped loudly in a sudden and desperate attempt to get her breath back, and as her lungs filled the fires began to subside and the roaring of the crowd returned.

Suddenly the contest was at an end. The gladiator with the plumed helmet held the sharp edge of his sword victoriously across the throat of his fallen opponent. He stared up to the crowd, waiting for their decision, staying his action until they voiced their command, showing that even in victory he was slave to their will. A woman climbed over the barrier between the arena and the tiered seating and pulled her dress off as she ran towards the two gladiators. The crowd roared as she lay down in front of them, opening her legs, stroking her wet cunt, offering herself, wanting only to be filled. Arria Sulla leant forward over the front of the box and shrieked her encouragement and Caristia, realising she had not been seen by her mistress, pulled her tunic down and wiped her sweat-streaked face with the back of her hand.

Two black slaves trained to keep the crowd in order ran from one of the entrances. They grabbed the woman by the ankles and started dragging her out of the arena. She fought against them, twisting in their powerful grip as she screamed to be left alone. They turned her over so that she was face down in the earth, and when they pulled her along her mouth filled with choking sand.

The crowd jeered at the black slaves, throwing food down on them to express their annoyance at being cheated of the show. There was a disturbance behind Caristia, and when she turned she saw a woman being passed above the crowd. She was a young yellow-haired Saxon and screaming with fear. The crowd lifted her above their heads and men fondled her breasts and thighs and ripped her clothes from her. She looked terrified. When they held her high by the side of Caristia she was wearing only tight silk panties. They were lemon-yellow with a seam running horizontally, just above the crease at the joining of her rounded buttocks and the tops of her lithe thighs. As she squirmed in the hands of her captors the material of the panties creased into the crack of her buttocks and twisted tightly between the valley of flesh that formed the cleft saddle between the tops of her thighs. One man splayed her legs wide and licked the outer labia squeezed around the tightly-pulled strip of material. She squealed as he reached up, pulled harshly at the barely covering material and drove his tongue into her cunt. Another turned her and, still with the first burying his tongue as deeply as he could between the material and the swelling flesh of her crack, started spanking her. Her protests grew louder but Caristia could see that, notwithstanding the rough treatment and the look of terror on her face, by the way she dropped her legs wider with each penetrating probe of the tongue, and the way she lifted her bottom towards the smacking hand, she wanted more.

All this time Innocenti stood as her mistress had commanded, still with her hands by her sides. Her tears had dried and turned to salt on the lower lids of her eyes. She had endured the noise of the crowd and their constant pushing, the sight of her mistress being taken by Fronto, Caristia's sobs of joy and the moans of the women in the arena, and still she had done the bidding of Arria Sulla. Caristia saw the fragile innocence on the girl's face and felt a wave of compassion. The crowd lurched as the young Saxon girl made a final bid for freedom. Everyone pushed at the same time and Innocenti was knocked sideways. Arria Sulla swung round, her face only minutes before enraptured with ecstasy, now darkened by the thunder clouds of anger.

'Still!' she screamed as if all the time she had been aware of Innocenti's obedience and now of her inadvertent defiance. 'Still! Still! Still!'

The tears welled up again in Innocenti's eyes, and as she tried to stand up straight and put her hands close to her sides, the crowd surged again and knocked her off balance. She fell against her mistress, looking in every direction with nervous, blinking eyes, but her desperate glances found no saviour.

'Impertinence! Impertinence!' roared Arria Sulla, her face reddening as she was overcome by an outburst of uncontrollable rage. 'Impertinence!' She pushed Innocenti away and brushed the front of her dress as if she had been contaminated by contact with the girl, or as if she was ridding herself of dust which had blown up on a sudden breeze. 'Bend over! Bend over!' she howled, still flicking her fingers down the thin material that covered her breasts.

Innocenti was still trying to stand to attention, still trying to please her seething mistress and, confused and frightened, she did not respond immediately to her new instruction. Caristia saw her bewilderment, and the sadness she felt for her when she'd seen her standing so obediently and unnoticed suddenly turned to unconsidered action. She could not believe what she was doing as she struggled free of the men, who were now fighting over the terrified Saxon girl, and stood between her mistress and her trembling prey.

'She could not help it, mistress,' she heard herself say, still driven by thoughtless momentum.

Arria Sulla froze. For a moment it was as if the world had stopped spinning on its axis. Then her face, already overtaken by wrath, was contorted by an unleashed fury. She stared at Caristia, for a moment speechless. Caristia fell back, filling with anxiety as she realised what she had done. She bit her lip and started shaking as abruptly, as though a sudden storm had broken, Arria Sulla grabbed her hair and twisted it in a knot around her clenching fingers. Caristia was spun around like a top as her enraged mistress kicked at her wildly.

'Take her! Beat her!' she spat at her male slaves, all the time kicking at Caristia. 'You! Take her over your knee. Slap her until she is bleating and then, when you are tired, give her to your fellow and let him take over. I do not want to hear the crowd above your beating hands!'

She twisted Caristia violently and flung her to the slaves. The first picked her up and, as his fellow pushed the crowd back from around them, took her over his knee and pulled up the hem of her tunic. She squirmed in a vain attempt to escape but she knew it was pointless. She felt the pressure of the top of his thigh as he pressed her down, holding her with a hand in the small of her back, taking aim, looking at his target.

'Get on with it!' screamed his mistress.

He smoothed his hand across Caristia's buttocks, letting his fingers trace around the tops of her thighs, looking at where they touched before opening them enough to expose the perfect oval of her cunt, shaved and naked. He opened her thighs more, revealing the bud of her clitoris. She brought her buttocks together slightly, almost a twitch. It was not an attempt to resist but an acknowledgment that she had given in to the punishment, that she knew it was unavoidable and that she was ready for the pain that would last as long as her mistress ordered. The huge African raised his hand, held it for a moment as again he looked at his target, then brought it down flatly across the tender skin of Caristia's bottom.

It smacked loudly. He did not carry through the blow but stopped it at the point of contact, letting the sound echo in his hand, not allowing it to be swallowed by taking the stroke further. It stung but it was not heavy. It burned but its weight did not mask the sharpness of skin against skin. As soon as the smack rang out he lifted his hand again, held it high, composed the target in his mind and brought it down again. She tightened as it landed and grimaced as the loud smack filled her ears. Again it came down and she shouted out, but she knew her cry would seem like a whimper compared to the shrieks that would follow. She knew this was only the start and that she had to suffer much more until her mistress would be satisfied that her punishment was adequate.

Caristia was hardly aware of the fighting around her, of the blonde Saxon girl being held by the group of men as others joined in and drove their cocks into her exposed cunt. She hardly heard the girl's screams as men finished in her sex, in her mouth and over her face and breasts. She reached down and gripped the African's leg; she needed something to hold on to, something to tighten against. She encircled his calf with both her hands and the warmth of his skin and the tension of his heavy muscles sent shivers up her arms. As each smack came down she tightened her grip more, but as she did her body filled not only with the burning pain of her punishment but with the excitement she felt in touching her tormentor's body. She rubbed her hands along his calf, feeling the back of his knee, then as the spanking continued she folded her head below his thigh and opened her mouth against his oiled skin. The next blow caused her to bite into his leg and the next to bite harder. She licked him between the blows but bit even harder as each one struck. She reached underneath his leg, finding first his heavy balls, then as she continued to bite his flesh she took hold of his stout cock. She lifted her bottom, burning more with each spank, and felt her own moisture on her thighs as, with each blow the punishment lifted her towards a final shuddering convulsion of overpowering ecstasy.

Caristia slid from the African's knee and slumped against the back of the box, gasping and panting as her orgasms, although receding, jolted through her like lightning from a passing storm. The Saxon girl was lying against a boarded partition with a man holding his cock in her mouth as he finished in long, spurting gushes of semen. A fanfare was blown and naked girls led out a procession from the main entrance at ground level. Fronto leant forward onto the rail of the box as, preceded by Sparton, Theogenes and several gladiators, Bec marched elegantly into the arena.

'What a beauty,' he said, trying to attract Sparton's attention. 'I must have her! Sparton!' he shouted impatiently. 'Sparton!'

Sparton heard his name and turned.

'Sparton, here!' repeated Fronto. 'Here!'

Sparton knew better than to ignore Lucretius Fronto, and ordering Theogenes to wait at the head of the procession, marched across the arena towards him.

'You have a beauty there that takes my eye, Sparton,' shouted Fronto. 'The black-haired animal with the fire in her eyes.'

Sparton laughed.

'She is an animal indeed, sir. I have been training her for her owner. She has responded well but she cannot be tamed.'

'Who is her owner, Sparton? I have to speak to him.'

'It is Olconio Rufo, sir. But he will not sell,' he said, turning to walk away. 'He has already refused many offers, sir. I do not think he will change his mind.'

'Bring her over. I must see her at close quarters.'

'The procession, sir. We must continue with the procession or the crowd will be angered,' said Sparton anxiously.

'The procession can wait,' insisted Fronto.

Sparton hesitated, but only for a moment; he was not going to argue with Fronto. He told three of the other gladiators to grab Bec and bring her over. She struggled against them, dropping low on bent legs and digging her heels into the ground. They pulled her forward as mounds of sand built in furrows around her heels. They held her in front of the box, a barely captive animal, her eyes ablaze with hatred. She saw Caristia and lurched forward, for a moment taking her captors by surprise and escaping their grip. Fronto pulled back in fear as the three gladiators rushed to recapture her. Caristia, still inflamed by the delights of her punishment, felt a wave of pleasure rush through her as she felt the focus of Bec's anger. It was as though the threat itself was enough to renew her ecstasy.

Fronto saw Rufo pushing his way through the crowds, worried at seeing his prize possession held at the edge of the arena. He was surprised when Fronto confronted him.

'Rufo! Rufo! I must have her! Name your price!' demanded Fronto.

'Lucretius Fronto. You have surprised me with your joke,' retorted Rufo.

'It is no joke Rufo. She is as good as mine. Tell me your price,' said Fronto, thumping one of his fists sharply into the palm of the other hand. 'Your price!'

'She is priceless, sir. Surely you would not begrudge an honest working man the joy of such a prize. She is my pension, sir.'

'Then you will live a life of poor retirement. Not only because you will no longer have your little tigress but because the tax collector will want his dues for all the years you have deceived him.'

Rufo's face changed from one of worried confidence to one of fear and dread, and he hung his head in the sudden dissipation of defeat. As soon as Fronto saw his threat had hit the target, he knew the tigress was his.

Chapter 9
The Forum Baths

Caristia looked up at the Temple of Jupiter, closed to the public for seventeen years since its structure had become unsafe after the great earthquake of 62 AD. Huge columns bore its huge roof, itself topped with a statue of Jupiter glaring down from its apex, and in the distance, behind him, sitting in the mist like a brooding giant in Jupiter's heavenly garden, the colossal mass of Vesuvius. A column of smoke rose from its centre and Caristia shivered as she imagined the mountain was an opening to hell and the smoke that ascended from its flattened cone was the breath of Satan himself.

'Caristia! Keep up!' shouted Arria Sulla as she marched ahead through the Forum. She held Innocenti on a thin leather lead attached to a leather collar buckled tightly around her neck, but Caristia was free.

She ran a few paces so she was right behind her mistress. She looked around, her sparkling blue eyes wide as she took in the activity around her. Tradesmen held out their wares to passers-by, slaves were beaten for tardiness or misbehaviour or simply because their mistress or master was bored. One man, grey-haired with a dark red toga, held a young slavegirl over his knee and spanked her publicly. Several people gathered around and watched as the pale skin of her bottom reddened under the harsh spanking. When he became tired he offered her to others, who were only too eager to take up the duty. She squirmed in pain as each one took a turn and they all laughed when, unable to take any more, she begged for mercy. Caristia dawdled, standing behind a marble pillar, watching until she realised she had been left behind again. She ran quickly to catch up before her mistress discovered she was missing.

They walked through the noisy throng until they reached the women's entrance to the Forum Baths, much smaller than the impressive grandeur of the Stabian Baths, but because of their proximity to the Forum, popular with all who wished to be seen. Also, unlike the segregation between men and women which was rigorously enforced at the Stabian Baths, those in charge of the Forum complex took a more liberal attitude. Arria Sulla instructed her Nubian slaves to wait outside.

They entered the dressing room and immediately Arria Sulla let go of Innocenti's lead and dropped her dress to the floor. She raised her arms and stretched. Caristia thought how beautiful she was; lithe, full-breasted with a flat stomach that led to the perfectly raised mound of her sex. She tensed her shapely buttocks, bringing them together so that a fine line separated them, disappearing at its upper end into the small of her gracefully curved back and at its lower end into the dark triangle that hid her flesh.

'You may undress,' she said casually to Caristia. 'Then you can undress this one that I have on a lead. I cannot trust her to do it herself.' Innocenti looked down in embarrassment. 'Get on with it!' shouted Arria Sulla.

Caristia undid the small clasps that held her tunic at her shoulders. The gauzy material slipped away, unveiling the nipples of her pert breasts, then as it fell, revealing her narrow waist and smooth stomach. The dress slipped past her shaved sex, over her legs and down around her ankles. She stood there for a moment, like a freshly exposed nymph, sensing Arria Sulla's envy of her youth, of her fragility, but most of all of her innocent humility.

Arria Sulla threw her head back haughtily, unclipped the lead from Innocenti's collar and stared hard at Caristia. Caristia had learnt to respond quickly when her mistress glared at her like that, and immediately she stepped out of the tunic that encircled her feet and started untying the ribbons that held Innocenti's pale pink smock. She felt Innocenti tremble, as though she had suffered so much she could feel nothing now except fear. Caristia stroked her shoulders as she undid the ribbons and Innocenti bit her lip as she fought back tears. Caristia drew the girl's dress down, allowing the backs of her fingers to rub against her nipples, letting them catch between her fingers, tightening slightly against them so that they had to tug to getaway. They were small but hard and pink, and they sprang back as each one was caught then released. Caristia knelt and started to take the dress down over Innocenti's hips. She did not need to, it would have fallen easily, but Caristia wanted to look closely at the sex lips now in front of her face. She wanted a reason to linger, to see them revealed, to feel their gentle heat, to inhale their delicate scent.

The flesh was perfectly shaved, not a wisp of hair remained, it was completely smooth. The sight of it, so close, so delicate, caused Caristia to catch her breath. She moved her face towards it and her mouth opened; she could not help herself. She inhaled the sweet fragrance that arose from the contours. She wanted to press her cheeks against it, to its perfume filling her nostrils. She held Innocenti's dress around the girl's thighs, not allowing it to fall, maintaining the spell a little longer, holding onto the delightful anticipation of her nakedness, capturing the present as if she was freezing time.

She wanted to lick, to taste Innocenti's fragrance, saturating her senses. She reached forward a little, urging herself towards the fleshy cleft, the close folds that allowed only the slightest sight of the hidden clitoris. Only the faintest darkening of the soft pink hue as it led towards the enclosed, moist interior. Caristia felt a wave of anxiety, as if her desires had turned to fear, as if the loss of this moment would bring destruction, as if she was exposed on the edge of an abyss.

Suddenly the spell was broken as Arria Sulla yanked Innocenti's lead. The girl toppled sideways and choked as her mistress pulled insistently on the tight leash. Her dress was ripped from Caristia's hands, and tore before she could let it go. Arria Sulla kicked out aggressively at Caristia.

'I said undress her, slut. Not put your tongue inside her. Look, your little lover is in tears. Perhaps it is passion. Perhaps she has not yet had enough of your attention.' She yanked the lead again and scowled at Innocenti. 'Bend over girl! Your little friend is going to punish you for letting her down. You see, she wanted to lick you, to fondle you and you pulled away, and so abruptly. Yes, you do deserve to feel the heat of her hand. Here! Over this bench!'

Arria Sulla pulled Innocenti over to a smooth marble bench, its white edges glistening and wet. Innocenti stumbled sideways, looking back at her mistress only for a second before she knelt on the mosaic floor and bent obediently across the wide bench. Her small breasts squashed against the cold surface as she stretched her arms forward compliantly and gripped the opposite edge with her fingers. Her narrow back blended with the oyster-white marble but her fragile form was picked out in all its features by soft shadows in the hollow of her back, between her shoulder blades and the dark valley of her buttocks.

'You shall use this,' said Arria Sulla, handing Caristia a flat leather blade, about the length of Caristia's arm and the width of her hand. It was shaped into a handle at one end, and when Caristia wrapped her fingers around it the weight of the blade made its length spring in her hand. 'And you shall know what it is like to be a mistress. Now begin. I will watch and check that you do it correctly, and if you do not then it will be the worse for you, and your little friend.'

Arria Sulla reached down and took Caristia's left nipple between her finger and thumb. She squeezed hard then twisted it until Caristia opened her mouth to cry out. Arria Sulla let go and laughed. Several other women gathered around and watched as Caristia stood nervously behind Innocenti's exposed bottom.

She held the leather paddle in her right hand, tipping it slightly to feel its weight before lifting it back. She saw Innocenti's bottom tighten in anticipation. She knew what it felt like, that moment before the smack landed, that second of waiting before the swish of air and the slap of contact. She wanted to be in Innocenti's place, she wanted to tip her own bottom up as she heard the leather cutting the air, and she wanted to tighten her buttocks together, to narrow the dark cleft between them as much as possible so that when it landed she could absorb all its fire.

Innocenti did not move when Caristia brought it down the first time. Perhaps it was not hard enough, she thought. Perhaps she had held back. The second blow was more powerful; she held her arm in the air longer and took aim with more care. When she drew back it left a panel of redness, the same shape as the paddle, across the girl's pale skin. The next blow she brought down with intention, with a determination to redden the skin even more, to double up the fire that had already started. The next she brought down quickly, hardly allowing her hand to pause before she pulled it back towards its target. She felt her chest tightening as it swept down, tensing herself so she could put all her power into it. The smack was like a screech in her ears and, as Innocenti jolted beneath the blow, Caristia felt a wave of delight spreading deep within her. The next was even harder and Innocenti yelped, the next harder still and, with the next as hard as she could make it, Caristia felt a warm flow of moisture wetting her thighs and cooling the swollen flesh of her heated labia.

Innocenti jerked with each blow, her fingers tightening against the edge of the marble bench, the skin of her bottom and the backs of her thighs reddening as though on fire. Caristia saw from the corner of her eye her own hardened nipples, and they began to ache as though her witnessing their tension was a signal for their increased sensitivity. The women looked on, urging Caristia to hit harder, bending down and looking at Innocenti's face, watching her biting her lips, witnessing her squeezing her eyelids tightly, analysing her expression, examining her suffering. Caristia wanted to kneel behind her victim, she wanted to open her legs and rub her own cunt across the skin of the girl's bottom, to feel its heat, to absorb its pain, to cover it with her own passionate wetness. She wanted to lick it, she wanted to open the girl's legs and delve the tip of her tongue into the wet centre of her victim's juicy vagina.

Caristia dropped the paddle to the ground and straddled Innocenti. She felt the heat from the girl's reddened bottom rising between her legs, meeting the wetness of her flesh. She reached down and placed her hands into the small of Innocenti's back, pressing her harder against the bench as she lowered herself. She felt the contact of the red skin of Innocenti's bottom as it touched her swollen cunt and, as her body filled with the girl's heat her eyes closed. She rubbed her sex against the girl's bottom, forward and back to expose her own hardened clitoris, side to side to open and expose the moist centre of her slit.

She felt Innocenti lifting her bottom, responding to her touch, and Caristia dropped forward and laid her tongue against Innocenti's neck. She tasted her skin and, as Caristia arched her back and forced her exposed clitoris against the red buttocks beneath it, she felt a wave of delight running within her. It arose from her clitoris like a single flame and quickly spread throughout her body like a fire borne on a tempest. She licked the girl's neck again but her excitement was too great, she could delay no longer. She reared up as her orgasm gripped her, contorted her in a vicious seizure and forced her to arch her back in an ever-tightening convulsion of unstoppable delight.

'Stop!' shrieked Arria Sulla. 'Stop!' Caristia hardly heard her. 'Stop!' Arria Sulla screamed in a frenzy as she grabbed Caristia's hair and pulled her off Innocenti. 'You act as though you are the girl's mistress!' she shrieked. She flung her to the floor and kicked her. 'You are a wilful bitch. Driven more by the heat between your legs than the orders of your mistress. Do you want me to toss you into the street?'

'Mistress. Please forgive me. I thought—'

'You thought!' Arria Sulla's face reddened with rage. 'You do not think! You serve!'

She grabbed Caristia's hair again and pulled her to her feet. She slapped her sharply across the face then bent her across her knee, folded an arm around her waist and underneath her stomach, and smacked her bare bottom hard. Caristia winced but the pain was not enough to take the pleasure she had felt with Innocenti away. Arria Sulla smacked her until her hand was sore, but even though Caristia relaxed her buttocks, opening the dark fissure between them and exposing the shape of her sex lips, it was not enough to divert her from the delight she had just experienced. Arria Sulla sensed it, pursed her lips and dropped her slave to the floor.

She grabbed Innocenti's lead and ordered Caristia to follow. They went through a broad arch into the coolest room, the frigidarium, and Arria Sulla plunged into the cold water pool at its centre. Caristia and Innocenti stood silently by the side of the pool, neither daring to look up. As Arria Sulla climbed out her smooth skin was goose-pimpled and her nipples were shrunken and hard. She threw her auburn hair back and the cold water arced in a rainbow as it glittered in the light that flooded in through the high open roof. Still naked she grabbed Innocenti's lead and marched through another arch into the first warm room, the tepidarium, then through a heavy door into the hottest, the calidarium. Caristia gasped as a waft of heat hit her face. It stung like a smack and took her breath away. Women reclined on benches around the walls, naked and covered with sweat as their servants attended them, oiling their skin, cleaning them, offering them goblets of wine, licking their nipples and some extending their tongues between their legs. Two women lay on a marble bench, each with their tongue delving the other's cunt, their legs entwined around each other's head, squirming with passion, consuming each other's heat. Caristia watched them and listened to their moans as one, the younger of the two, looked up and caught her eye, before slipping her tongue back into the pink slit of her companion's fleshy vagina.

Arria Sulla made her way to the back of the tepidarium and entered a dark passageway. She glowered at Caristia to follow, and yanked Innocenti's lead when she held back fearfully. Caristia could hardly see as she fumbled her way along the dark tunnel. It was a duct for the hot air that came from the fires below, and was even hotter than the calidarium. Her feet felt as if they were burning and she screwed up her toes to keep back the pain. They emerged into another hot room - the men's calidarium. Female slaves attended to the men who reclined on stone benches, most naked but some with togas draped across their shoulders and some with towels around their waists. Two girls sat at the feet of one, reaching up as they oiled his body, embrocating every part of his flesh, rubbing oil into his erect cock, licking along its venous length and sucking its swollen glans. Another nearby was washing her master, ladling cool water over his body then rubbing him with fragrant oils. One man, lean and grey-haired, stood in a pool of water up to his waist. Two naked girls, both short-haired and small-breasted, kept plunging beneath the surface, tipping their bottoms up as they dived, taking it in turn to suck his cock until, still giggling, they had to return to the surface.

'Madam Sulla,' said the man easing himself up onto the side of the pool. 'I see you have brought some entertainment.'

'Severus, I have brought a slave with an appetite for pleasure but who needs a lesson in obedience.'

Severus laughed as one of the girls sucking his cock pushed her friend away and latched her full lips around its burgeoning tip.

'Then perhaps you would like me to take a hand in her discipline. I have never yet failed to curb the desires of a disobedient slave.'

'You may try, sir, but I warn you, she has a strong appetite.'

'Set her in the water here and we shall see how strong her appetite is!'

He pushed away the girl who was sucking him.

'Caristia,' said Arria Sulla coldly, 'get in the water. You have a new master to please; Severus. Let us see if he can make you more responsive to my orders.'

She snatched the lead that led to the collar around Innocenti's neck as Caristia dipped her toe into the water. It felt cold in the hot air and she pulled it out again, shivering. The two girls with Severus giggled, but when he scowled at them they stopped obediently and looked down.

'I see what you mean, madam. Already she disobeys you. And with such a simple instruction. Girl!' he shouted. 'Get in the water! Now!'

Caristia did not hesitate, his tone so forceful, his orders clearly to be followed. She reached her foot into the cold water again, bent her knees, then reaching behind her and gripping the side of the pool, she slipped into the ice-cold water. It chilled her body and her nipples hardened as waves splashed against them. She felt the outer flesh of her cunt contracting and the pressure squeezed against the tip of her clitoris, making it retract even deeper behind its protective covering. She stood on tiptoe and the water settled just below her breasts, She dropped her gaze and stood before Severus.

'What a pretty mouth you have,' he said as he reached out and circled it with his fingers. 'Open it, child. Let me see its size and shape.' She did as she was told and stood stiffly in the water while he scrutinized her. Goose-pimples surrounded her shrunken nipples and there was a tinge of blueness around her mouth and beneath her eyes. 'Good. Now, and I make my instructions clear, bend down and place that pretty mouth around my member. It is hard and thick, as you will find out, but you will get it in. Then, when you have your lips sealed around it you must lick with your tongue, along the sensitive underside. And suck it. Yes, and suck it diligently. I want to feel the tip of your tongue and the pressure of your cheeks as you encourage it to fill you with its goodness. I want you to take it into the back of your mouth, so that when you extract its precious liquid it does not pause on your tongue but goes straight down your throat.'

He lifted her chin in his hand, then without further warning he clasped the top of her head and thrust it onto his stiff cock. Water burst around her ears as she fought to keep from overbalancing. She opened her mouth, and with his hands still on her head he directed her face towards it. She took his cock in and immediately felt it swelling against the insides of her cheeks as she sucked as conscientiously as she could. Severus pressed her onto it, thrusting its tip in deeper as, doing as he ordered, she ran her tongue along its underside, feeling the sensitive skin that covered it, licking the raised veins that pulsated along its length. She felt it touch the back of her throat. She pulled back but his hands held her. She did not hesitate and took his cock to the back of her throat. She felt the throbbing glans pressing against it; pulsating, filling, plugging. She licked it and sucked it and felt its length beating with his orgasm.

She threw her head back. Her wet hair fell behind her in thick long strands and her bright blue eyes, barely open, sparkled in the luminous flashes that came off the turbulent water. She looked faint and hopeless, then instead of waiting to be forced back she opened her eyes wide, tipped herself forward and fixed her mouth around his throbbing stem. She knew her bottom was above the surface of the water, she could feel the air against it, then she felt his smacking hand and, with a sudden eager gulp, his cock was into the back of her throat. She held it there and with each wet spank that fell on her upturned bottom she took it deeper, allowing it to swell so much it would not move. Then as his semen surged up its length, she let it spray into her swallowing throat. She drew it all out, drinking his essence as he continued to spank her in a confusion of water and bubbles.

But the spanking did not end. She had barely drawn a breath, and with his semen running down her throat, he forced her onto it again. His wet hand slapped her buttocks, pale and blue in the cold water, but mottled red where his palm had fallen. He gripped her with his arm folded around her waist, smacking her ten times before he released her for relief. Her head was filled with the noise of the water and the laughter of the men who had gathered around. Again he spanked her but this time she did not wriggle as much; this time she bent herself more willingly, stretching her arms around his hips, allowing her bottom to rise to his hand. When again he released her she did not pull back, but waited until he resumed her punishment.

She knew others were spanking her; she could feel the different weights, the different sizes of their hands, the different degrees of delightful pain they brought. The skin of her bottom was so tight and the cold water put out the flames of their spanking hands so quickly that there seemed no limit to the amount of punishment she could take. She revelled in the pain of each stroke, savouring the stinging as it mixed with the pleasure she drew from the semen that ran down her throat.

The others dragged her out, rolled her onto her back and took it in turns to fuck her. They put her onto all fours and took her from behind, sometimes making her suck another as they smacked her bottom at the same time as they finished. When they had all done with her they threw her into the pool, where she floated on her back until some slavegirls pulled her out.

She lay on the side, panting, gasping, and still shuddering from the finally easing of her orgasms. She looked around bleary-eyed and saw Fronto lying back on a marble chair, a girl lying across his knee while he rubbed her reddened bottom lazily with one hand and drank from a goblet he held in the other. He must have been there all the time. Arria Sulla pulled Innocenti's lead and marched over to him. He looked up, smiled and pushed the girl casually from his knee, sending her rolling onto the floor.

'Arria Sulla,' he said, getting up and looking first at the trembling Innocenti, and then across to Caristia, 'surely you have not come to do business.'

'I do not know what you mean sir,' she said, looking away from him and staring at Caristia.

'Well, I see you here, attended by your two little treasures, and I can only think that you have brought them to bargain with.'

'You have nothing that would interest me, Lucretius Fronto,' she said disdainfully.

'I think you are testing me with a joke, madam, but I will humour you. Come, I will show you what *does not* interest you.'

Arria Sulla bent down to Caristia and helped her to her feet. Caristia felt warmed by her mistress's patronage and stood up beside her. Fronto led the way into the open gymnasium at the rear. It was enclosed by a high wall and colonnaded on three sides with vertically ribbed, marble pillars. In the centre was Bec, wearing only a narrow leather thong pulled up tightly between her legs. Its thin gusset parted her sex, forcing the flesh of her labia to each side of the taut leather. She was restrained by two Nubians, each with a long pole with a ring at the end, one around her neck and the other around her waist. They struggled to hold her, and when she saw Caristia she grabbed the pole which led from her neck, twisted it and threw the Nubian holding it to the floor. Arria Sulla laughed loudly.

'I see your problem sir. Do you wish to borrow my male slaves to hold onto your little prize, or perhaps my two attendants would do better?'

She held her hand out towards Caristia and Innocenti. Fronto scowled. The Nubian struggled to his feet and pushed at the pole, keeping Bec at a distance but unable to restrain her violence.

'Madam, you are mistaken and your mocking tone is misplaced. I have had the tigress trained especially so that no one will be able to face her in the ring. That her guards cannot control her only tells me that her training has been a success. I do not think your little slaves should even be close to her, especially the one you call Caristia. See how my gladiator spits and snarls when she sees her. I think you should send her out of the gymnasium in case she is attacked.' He laughed, then walked up to Caristia and drove his hand between her naked thighs. The fierceness of his touch caused her to swallow hard. 'Yes, by the feel of her wet flesh, I think this little one is better suited to more moderate sports.'

Arria Sulla's annoyance was obvious. She screwed up her eyes and fixed Fronto with a piercing glare.

'I fear you are no judge of what it takes to survive in the ring, sir. I think my own little warrior would easily claim victory if you only had courage enough to allow the match.'

Fronto's eyes widened in amazement.

'Do I understand you correctly, madam? You are proposing a match between my fiery tigress and your fragile little slave?'

'Yes sir, I am.'

'Then madam, I accept.'

Chapter 10
A failed escape

The details of the contest had been agreed - it would be on 24 August in the Amphitheatre and, like many contests involving women, it would be held at night by the light of torches and braziers. Arria Sulla said the final 'special' rules would be announced on the day, and although Fronto was curious he was not concerned. A few days before the set date, Arria Sulla decided to take Caristia to the Temple of Isis so that the priests could bless her, as she did not want to run the risk that her contestant would be, in any way, under prepared.

Arria Sulla led Caristia into the small enclosed courtyard of the torch-lit temple. The priests stood huddled around the altar with the crowd of worshippers silently crammed together around them. Caristia squinted to see in the shimmering red hues cast by the burning torches, and saw something hanging above the altar. As they got closer she saw it was a young woman crouched in a small cage made from shiny metal bars. It was barely big enough for her to get into and her knees where thrust up beneath her chin. Her eyes were covered with a tight bound mask which extended down over her mouth, leaving only a hole around her nostrils. Her wrists were secured by silver manacles and her ankles chained so tightly that even if she was free she would not have been able to move them at all. The cage swung slowly on a plaid rope and, as it was caught by the red light of the torches, Caristia saw the angry red stripes that covered the girl's naked bottom.

The priests moved back as Arria Sulla approached. Innocenti was lying at their feet. She too was bound, her wrists tied behind her back with leather thongs and her ankles and knees bound with thin rope. She lay on her side, her knees slightly bent and her head craned back. Her hair had been plaited in two pigtails, each turned back on themselves and tied up with thin red cords, the looped ends sticking out slightly and at the same level as the lobes of her ears. She looked frail and elfin, abandoned and pitiful. Her dark eyes flickered as she caught sight of Arria Sulla. She opened her mouth slightly and licked out her tongue as if she had been waiting only for this moment, as if she had been trained to respond like this only to the approaching footsteps of her mistress. Arria Sulla stretched her foot out towards the captive girl and Innocenti licked it, slowly and with earnest passion, running the tip of her tongue upwards from between her mistress's toes to her slender ankle, and then back again.

'Good,' said Arria Sulla, smiling as she stretched out the other foot for Innocenti to lick. 'Good. Now, secure her; I have another who needs your attention.' Arria Sulla's two Nubian's lifted Innocenti away, but as they pulled her over to the temple entrance she kept her tongue against her mistress's foot for as long as she could. The Nubians held her while girls untied her wrists and secured them in front of her with leather thongs, pulling them as tight as they could, making her wince. They fixed a round wooden bar across her mouth and bound it securely behind her head. They left the thongs around her knees and ankles but checked they were tight. The Nubians lifted her up to a metal bar fixed between the main colonnades of the entrance and dropped the bindings at her wrists over a large hook attached to it. They left her hanging there, her feet clear of the ground, desperate and alone. Her body stretched under its own weight, accentuating her slender lines, her flat stomach and her narrow hips. Her breasts were flattened against her chest and the arch of her lower ribs tightened against her smooth skin. Caristia saw tears in the corners of her eyes as she bit into the wooden bar wedged firmly between her teeth.

The tallest of the priests stepped forward.

'Madam Sulla, state your request. The order of our lady Isis is at your service.'

'I want this slave blessed. She is to enter the ring and I want her to be guarded by Isis herself. You must make sure Queen Isis will be watching over her so she can secure victory for me.'

The priest looked at Caristia and smiled as, into the red glow of the torchlight, Fronto appeared with Drusus in attendance.

'Madam!' exclaimed Fronto as he bowed low with a flourish. 'I catch you at your prayers. You are indeed a devout follower of our Queen Isis. Come, we will worship together. Perhaps I can say a prayer for your little slave.'

'Yes, and I can say one for yours,' she responded curtly.

'Madam, you are too kind,' he mocked, taking her arm and leading her towards the altar. 'Look,' he said pointing to the girl trapped in the small cage high above their heads. 'Another one seeking a blessing. I hope your simple pleas work for your little gladiator. They will indeed need to bring about a miracle.'

'I think some prayers will suffice, sir. I do not demand miracles, nor do I need them.'

'Madam, you are so gentle to those that live only to obey you. But may I ask, has your kindness worked with your other little slave?' He poked Innocenti with a silver embossed cane. 'It would seem not, or presumably I would not find her like this.'

Arria Sulla scowled at Innocenti hanging on the iron bar with the wooden stave in her mouth. 'Priest,' she said, hardly able to contain her annoyance with Fronto. 'Priest!' She pointed at the girl in the cage. 'Would this be a proper blessing for my slave?'

'Yes indeed. It would madam.'

'Then arrange it!' she said, glancing sideways to make sure Fronto was watching. 'Caristia! Stand over there and wait. At attention!'

Caristia stepped aside and stood with her hands by her sides as some of the worshippers began lowering the cage. Men pressed around her, touching her, feeling her breasts and slipping their fingers between her thighs. She stood as still as possible, not allowing their pinching fingers to distract from her instructions, but their probing made it almost impossible. She screwed up her eyes, trying to concentrate. Suddenly she felt the warmth of someone's mouth against the side of her face, then she heard softly spoken words in her ear. It was Drusus. 'My sweet, sweet Caristia,' he said softly. 'I cannot bear to see you suffering like this.'

Just the sound of his voice set her heart racing. She stiffened her arms by her sides, afraid in case Arria Sulla would see her quaking with excitement. 'Drusus,' she whispered, hardly opening her mouth, 'is that really you?'

'My sweet,' he replied, pressing his lips against her cheek. 'I must be quick. I do not know how long my master will stay. He is obsessed with his new possession. Bec, she is called, a vicious gladiator who no one can control. Everyone fears her. I feel pity for whoever she faces in the ring.'

Caristia bit her lip, frightened by his words, as if suddenly a fresh certainty had been added to her existing fear.

'It is me,' she said with a trembling voice. 'I am to face this tigress.'

Drusus looked at her blankly, stunned.

'This cannot be true,' he said falteringly. 'You are not a gladiator. You cannot be matched with this animal they say is from hell. Sweet Caristia, tell me this is not true.'

'But it is, my sweet,' she said, still standing to attention and looking forward obediently. 'The date has been arranged. We will meet at night by torchlight in the Amphitheatre. I fear I will die. How can it be otherwise? You have just told me my opponent is indomitable.'

'Then...' he hesitated as Arria Sulla's slaves approached. Caristia pushed her hands down stiffly by her sides, hoping her mistress had not seen her talking. 'Then,' he said, starting to speak quickly, 'we must find a way to be together. Caristia, we must...'

Before he could say any more the Nubians yanked him away, throwing him down and kicking him viciously. His head rocked to the side as one foot clubbed him squarely on the temple and he curled up in agony as another jabbed into his stomach.

Caristia looked down at him, ignoring the hands that were still pawing her, and tried to smile, but she did not know whether he saw her before she felt herself lifted and carried towards the now empty cage.

The one end was its door and they forced her down onto her knees in front of it. Hands pressed on her back so that her head was level with the top of the opening. The cage, constructed from heavy iron bars, was about knee high, the same width and a little longer in length. Caristia looked into it with fear; she could not believe there was enough room for anyone to get inside. A hand slapped her bottom, it felt almost playful - light, isolated, unmotivated - but when it landed again, and then again, she realised it was filled with painful purpose. She winced as her bottom burned with the harsh contact, then as it got harder she was prodded with something sharp and forced to crawl forward into the iron prison she was bowed before.

Her head dipped beneath the bar that formed the top of the entrance, all the time her bottom feeling the spanking that came in strong, rhythmic slaps. The spanking and the sharp prodding drove her forward, crawling, her elbows bent, her hands on the floor in front of her face. At the end a middle bar was fashioned into a circle. She knew that was where she must put her head and, before she even thought her knees had gained entry, her head was poking through the hole. The spanking continued, driving her still forward, squeezing her within the bars of the cage, cramming her tightly inside as she was crushed tighter into the confining prison of iron.

With her head through the hole and her shoulders pressed against the bars, the door was pushed together behind her. She felt a bar beneath her bottom pressing against the backs of her thighs as they squeezed the door shut behind her. She sensed her bottom was still exposed, poking out, captive and available to anyone, and she felt her hips pressed against the bars at the sides like an encompassing girdle of iron. She could not turn her head and she strained her eyes sideways to see what was happening: Men gathered around, reached into the cage and pulled her arms back, first leading them out over a central bar at the top of the cage, then pushing them back in again so that her weight was thrown onto her neck. They clamped a heavy shackle on each of her wrists and attached them to the bars at the side. She strained her back and lifted her head slightly, but the effort was too great and she dropped back onto the metal circle around her neck.

Caristia saw the shadow of the timber tripod that she'd seen when suffering on the altar. Its gaunt shape frightened her as it was contorted in the torchlight into the shape of a horny talon. The braided rope dangled menacingly from the apex of the tripod and the pulley block swung heavily at its end. When she heard a metallic thud close to her back, and saw the swinging shadow tighten as if it was in pain, she knew what was going to happen. Men leant back and hauled the rope through the pulley and the cage tipped sideways as it was yanked off the ground. Caristia gasped and tightened her eyes as it began to sway. She saw Innocenti still hanging from the metal rail, her eyes wide and her mouth clamped around the wooden bar in her mouth. One of the priests was standing behind her beating her buttocks with a long cane. Innocenti twisted on her bonds and the red stripes the cane was laying on her skin looked like fiery brands in the torchlight. The cage began to spin and Caristia lost sight of the suffering girl, but she imagined her stifled screams locked behind the wooden stave in her mouth.

Caristia was giddy by the time the cage hit the pulley block and was brought abruptly to a halt. She knew it had stopped but her dizziness meant the torches spun around her as if they were being carried around the temple enclosure by runners. She hung above the altar, staring down with her head fixed in the hole at the front of the cage and her bottom exposed at the back. She tried to move but the weight of her body against the opening around her neck and the way her arms had been tied made it impossible. She felt something against her buttocks, a touch of something thin like the long nail of a lover. It was a cane. As it was drawn across her skin she felt it touch the exposed flesh of her sex, which was squashed between the inviting indentation where the tops of her thighs met the lower part of her upturned buttocks. The cane was lifted, repositioned and pulled across her skin again, and this time it tugged slightly on the soft flesh of her labia. It was the lightest touch, but it was enough to lift the flesh slightly and expose the merest glimpse of the inner pinkness, and the glancing coolness that it brought, the sensation of her opening flesh, heralded a sliver of moistness to the freshly exposed surface.

The altar was still spinning below her face when the cane bit for the first time. She knew what was going to happen when it was lifted away from her skin, she knew it would come back hard, but when it landed on her bottom she was not prepared for the pain it brought. It was so sharp, so intense, that for the first few moments after it struck she did nothing. Her senses were mesmerized, then as the cutting pain penetrated she felt the full effect of its piercing impact. Her whole body tightened, her knees pressed harder against the side bars, her back lifted against the top and her buttocks tightened, but nothing absorbed the pain. She screwed up her face, tightening her eyes, but her confinement held in the pain and allowed her no relief. She did not feel the cane lifted away; the stinging shock remained even when it did not touch her, but when it came down again she felt its impact. The sting cut into her labia, burning, setting them on fire, but as she tightened against it again and prepared for the next she knew that when it landed her flesh would be more receptive to it, more punished by it.

Each blow increased the pain and with each strike her labia swelled, exposed for more punishment. She looked down at the altar and as the speed of the cane built to a crescendo, she felt her orgasm bursting within her captive body. A convulsing climax tore through her, forcing her even tighter against the bars, shaking her imprisoned body at its core and when finally, like an erupting volcano it exploded within her, she screamed in a blubbering shriek that filled the temple enclosure and continued until she had no breath left to feed it.

The cage was pulled forward at an angle on the rope and held there so that her face was above the centre of the altar. Her ears filled with the beating of her heart and she panted as excitement ran through her in ripples of confused exhilaration. She felt hands on her bottom, opening her cheeks wide, then she felt something against her anus, something cool and unforgiving. A rod, made from rolled leather and covered with closely napped suede, was attached with leather thongs to the rear bar of the cage and its rounded end placed against her exposed anus. The shaft was heavily ribbed, as thick as the thickest cock and half as long again. She felt her anus tighten as the leather rod's blunt end pushed against the tight muscular ring. For a moment the cage slipped slightly backwards and she felt the increased pressure as the tip began to prise open her anus, but just as it was penetrating her and her mouth dropped open, the cage was pulled back again and the pressure was relieved.

One of the priests mounted the altar and stood with his hips immediately in front of her face. His embroidered gold robe flowed loosely around him and flashed with the redness of the flickering torches. He opened the front and showed his naked, shaved body. His skin was oiled and glistened as if covered with a layer of precious metal. His cock hung loosely between his heavy balls and, when he cradled them, it bent over the front edge of his hand. Caristia gaped at him as he lifted his flaccid cock towards her and placed its bulbous end against her wet lips. She allowed it inside, feeling its heat, letting the glans rest on her tongue. She closed her lips around it and felt the pliable shaft beating with expectation. She sucked it and felt the hardening surface swelling. She sucked again, holding the shaft firmly in her encircling lips, and felt it lengthening as the glans enlarged and pressed further back on her tongue. She licked its underside and felt the veins beneath the silky skin throbbing, and as she moved her tongue around the rim of the glans she felt it push past and touch the back of her throat. It made her gag and she pulled back, slipping her mouth back along the shaft towards its end. The moment she pulled back she felt the pressure of the leather rod against her anus and realised the cage was no longer supported at an angle on the rope by anything other than her grasp on the priest's cock. Frantically she sucked it, drawing herself along its length until again it rested against the back of her throat and the pressure on her anus was eased.

But as she held it tightly between her lips she felt it hardening more, and with each pulsating throb it lengthened so that, unless she took it in deeper, it allowed the cage to fall back and the end of the rod to penetrate her anus. She sucked the priest's cock, gripping it with her lips as it thickened and lengthened, and still she dropped back against the unforgiving rod of leather. She felt her anus opening to it, encircling it tightly as it pushed against her and she sucked harder. She held it there for as long as she could, keeping the rod only at the entrance to her rectum, but suddenly she let the priest's cock slip back, gripping behind the flange of his glans with her tight lips. The cage fell back instantly and the rigid rod entered her deeply, filling her, stuffing her with its length and bulk. Quickly she sucked the cock in again and the rod in her rectum came out, but only slightly, only enough to feel a couple of its heavy ribs squeezing past the muscular ring that held it. She sucked desperately on the cock, but as it poured its hot semen into her she could not keep it in. When she released it again she could not even keep the helmet between her lips, and the rod buried its full length past her stretched anus as the cock ejaculated across her face.

The priest stepped aside and another took his place. Caristia managed to suck his cock in deeply and the rod slowly pulled out, rib by rib, until it was only just inside her bottom, but she could not keep it out for long. Each swallow, each suck, each tightening of her cheeks made her slide along the length of the leather implement, allowing it to ease itself slightly out. But each pause, each tightening pull of her flesh against the velvety leather made her ache for her own climax, made her body throb for a blissful conclusion. She did not have to wait many moments beyond the first longing. She felt it building inside her constrained body, at first unable to burst free then, when it started and she could not move with it, could not liberate it with a convulsion, a jerk, a frantic display of abandon, she simply let the cock in her mouth go free. As her face was again covered in hot semen, the penetration in her rectum was full and complete and the flames of her orgasm burned throughout her whole unmoving body.

They pulled the rod from her, easing it out over each of its ribs, then released the shackles from the bars and drew her out of the cage. She did not want to come out at first and twisted her head so she was jammed tightly, but they held the flesh of her labia, pinching it and gripped her hips, and poked her breasts with sticks until finally she was free. The priest in the gold robe sat on a carved throne by the altar and ordered the men to lift her and place her across his knee. She felt her nipples between their fingers as they did, and although they were already firm and prominent she felt them throbbing as they hardened even more under the rough handling. The shackles on her wrists hung down heavily, her arms felt stiff from being bent back over the bars of the cage and when, finally, she was held face down above his knees, she sighed with the anticipation of relief. He opened his robe so that she lay against his naked flesh and, as she was draped across the tops of his thighs, bent at the hips with her feet just touching the ground, she felt the heat of his cock against her narrow waist.

'Now bless her with the pain of your hand, priest!' shouted Arria Sulla as she stood closely in front of Caristia's head. 'I want to see her buttocks glowing with your consecration.'

Caristia looked up and saw that Arria Sulla's dress was undone down the front and her naked body beneath was fully exposed. Caristia watched her hand run down her flat stomach, then as it slowed, she watched her mistress's fingers probe between her trimmed pubic hair. She parted it and with two fingers opened the soft folds of her cunt, then she circled the clitoris and teased it out. As Caristia watched her mistress's exposed slit so closely, she felt a building heat in the swollen flesh of her own sex. It was as if her mistress was massaging *her*, as if she was exciting *her* throbbing clitoris.

The priest circled his hand across Caristia's bottom, dragging his finger around, tracing her buttocks then running a fingertip between the valley that separated them. He opened her legs slightly, pressing lightly between the tops of her thighs until the shape of her shaved sex was revealed. He ran his finger along its centre and her outer labia parted in a moist pink line of expectant, satiny softness.

'Get on with it!' shouted Arria Sulla, half closing her eyes and biting her lip to try and hold on to her excitement as she ran her fingers deeper into her wetness.

The priest's circling hand drew away from Caristia's bottom and there was a momentary pause, a silent gap of nothingness, as though the universe was hesitating on the brink of something unknown. Everything was silent and Caristia's mind, although seeing Arria Sulla's moist flesh in front of her eyes, plugged the gap with images of freedom, of sunlight, of Drusus, then as the lull was interrupted the fantasies disappeared and her head was filled with the blazing fires of pain.

His hand spanked hard, not stopping after it had struck but continuing until her buttocks had absorbed all its momentum. Arria Sulla leant back and squeezed her fingers around her clitoris, as if the blow on Caristia's bottom had filled her with energy, with an expectation that could only be discharged by her own pulsating flesh. It rose to her touch, a hardened nipple of joy, poking between the glistening spread of her moist labia. Caristia wanted to lick and touch, to taste, to suck. The priest's hand came down again, harder, and Caristia threw her head back in agony. Arria Sulla opened her legs more and pushed her hips forward, Caristia's nostrils filling with the musky scent of her mistress, and she inhaled deeply as the priest's hand came down again.

Arria Sulla moved closer to her suffering slave, opening her legs wide, spreading her lower lips, pressing her hips forward so that the soft flesh squeezed between her fingers, and the erect clitoris touched Caristia's lips. Caristia opened her mouth and let her tongue reach out. She tasted the moisture, and like the scent of rain on a summer's day, it filled her body with its soft fragrance. Another spanking blow made her gasp but she did not move her face; she was like a bee drinking nectar and she opened her mouth wider and let her tongue reach inside the moist petals. She tasted the inner wetness, stronger against her probing tongue. Then when the hand struck again on her stinging buttocks she sucked, drinking in the wetness, allowing it to run on her tongue and trickle down her parched throat.

Caristia craned her neck back as Arria Sulla bent forward, resting her hands in the small of Caristia's back and abandoning her cunt to her slave's ravenous mouth. Caristia lapped at it, pressing her nose against her mistress's clitoris, inhaling its fragrance, absorbing its moisture as she delved her tongue as deep into the silky flesh as she could. Arria Sulla watched the hand beating her slave's bottom, she scrutinised the increasing redness covering the pale skin, then as her cunt sent shockwaves into her hips and up into her chest, she dropped her face forward between Caristia's buttocks and drove her tongue into the girl's anus. Caristia gasped, the sudden cessation of the spanking and her mistress's wriggling tongue shocking her, filling her and setting her on fire. She lifted her buttocks to get all she could, opening them wide, allowing Arria Sulla's tongue to go deep, but as the tip probed she felt her orgasm overcoming her. She tightened and the tension pulled her back. She could barely reach Arria Sulla's cunt any more but it did not matter. All she could feel was her mistress's tongue, its searching tip and the heat and the fire of passion as her orgasm, like a storm of flames, ran through her shaking body.

Caristia crouched, exhausted on the cold mosaic floor. She sat up slowly, putting her weight alternately on each buttock to try and ease the pain which still stung her. She stretched out her legs to alleviate their stiffness, leant back against a massive column and dropped her hands onto her thighs. Drusus, barely visible in the shadows where he had been hiding, reached around the column and touched her shoulder. She could tell it was him straight away, but still she jumped.

'Caristia,' he whispered urgently, 'I will not let you suffer any more. We will escape together. I have heard that south of here, across an ocean, there is a vast desert where Arabs hold their women in great esteem and would take us in and treat us like themselves. We would no longer be slaves. Caristia! We would be free.'

'When, my sweet,' she said shakily. 'When can we go?'

'Now!' he said emphatically as he took her arm, pulled her to her feet and dragged her behind the column.

'But what about Innocenti?' she said, looking at the girl still trussed up, hanging from the metal rail with the wooden bar jammed between her teeth. 'We cannot leave her like that.'

'Then quickly,' he said, aware of the procession of worshippers coming closer and aware of the light of their torches exposing them to the danger of discovery.

Caristia strained up, but could not reach the leather thongs that held Innocenti on the metal bar. Drusus lifted her, holding her waist, and she managed to unbind Innocenti's wrists. The girl fell limply into her arms, as if she was asleep, unable to move, as if she had lost her will to carry on. She looked up at Caristia and a faint smile crossed her pale lips.

'Innocenti! Innocenti! Wake up. We can escape. Innocenti!' But Caristia's appeals were lost as the worshippers saw her and pulled the half conscious girl out of her grasp.

Innocenti's expression, only slowly waking to the possibility of freedom, suddenly dropped. The look of anticipation was stolen from her as she closed her eyes, submitted to the darkness that foreshadowed what would now befall her. She dropped to the floor and a heavy ring was clipped to her collar and a shackle to her wrist. Caristia stared down at her, crumpled and lying on her side, her hands flat together, tucked beneath her head as if in prayer. The curve of her narrow hips ran in a sweeping valley to the summit of her shoulders, then descended again to the elegant slope of her neck, its line broken only by the encircling collar. One knee covered the other and her legs were slightly bent so that the shape of her bottom was fully exposed. At the base of her flat stomach, where the darkness of shadow took over, there was nothing to be seen of her perfectly shaped sex, but the phantom image of it, hidden in shade, was as exciting to Caristia's eyes as the sight of it itself.

Drusus reached out to Caristia, hoping there was still time, that they could still avoid capture, but it was too late; attempting to rescue Innocenti had been their downfall. Caristia shrank back against the enveloping crowd but Drusus was held and pulled before an enraged Fronto.

'Take my ungrateful slave to the Gymnasium,' he shouted as he dispensed his summary justice. 'Put him in chains and leave him for tomorrow's sun. Give him no water and let him burn.'

Caristia stared after him as he was dragged away. He glanced back, his face filled with anguish, but he should not have turned and was whipped across the back by one of Fronto's more obedient slaves, and made to march forward to his punishment. As he disappeared, flinching under the pain of the merciless whip, he took with him any hope Caristia had left.

Chapter 11
Shame in the streets of Pompeii

There was no point in calling after Drusus; they pulled him away too quickly and by the time Caristia had realised what was happening she had been chained by the neck and dragged out of the Temple of Isis. When they hauled her under the high arched entrance of the House of the Gladiators her sweating, naked body was covered in dust and grime. She was thrown down on the sandy ground and, as she looked up through dirt-encrusted eyes, she saw the muscular legs of Sparton standing before her.

She stared upwards, following the tight bindings of leather that encircled his calves and knees, then up the bronzed thickness of his thighs until, finally, she saw the tight material that enveloped his heavy genitals and finished pulled up high onto his waist. He held out his foot it in front of her face. 'Kiss it before you rise, slave,' he said arrogantly.

Caristia flicked out her tongue and ran its tip along the top of his foot. She inhaled the strong scent of leather that rose from his dusty sandals. Her tongue dried as she licked his skin and he kicked her away impatiently.

'Do not be too rough with her Sparton,' said Arria Sulla. 'We do not want to diminish her charms.' She straddled Caristia, putting one foot either side of her naked waist, then bending and circling her fingers around Caristia's buttocks. 'Rather, I think, something which warms this beautiful bottom will both punish and prepare her better for what is in store.'

Caristia crawled back towards Sparton's foot, eager to please him, frightened by the surroundings and the menace in Arria Sulla's words.

'She is a pretty thing, madam. Too pretty for the ring, I fancy.' Caristia ran her tongue along the tops of his bare toes, tasting the salt between them and picking up the dust onto her lips. 'And, I think, too eager to satisfy her own pleasures.' He cocked his head to the side, smiled at the gladiators who stood around, and spoke mockingly. 'Look, she has not stood up. Already she forgets the instructions of her new master. Madam, this grovelling slave certainly needs discipline.'

He reached down, encircled her waist with his muscular forearm then lifted her off the ground, forcing her head and shoulders between his legs while lifting her bottom until level with his navel. Surprised and disorientated, she kicked her legs frantically in all directions but Sparton only laughed. She reached out for the ground, hoping to steady herself, but as her fingers touched it Sparton began walking around the enclosure, strutting in front of the gladiators assembled there, showing them his captive, eager to amuse them. Caristia squirmed frantically but his grip did not ease and her writhing only increased the entertainment. She was filled with a deep sense of humiliation.

'You see,' Sparton pronounced to the gladiators, 'our new gladiator cries out for a lesson in discipline. And of course our Lady Sulla is right; reddening her buttocks will bring her to heel.'

The gladiators laughed, one of them stepped forward and smacked Caristia's bottom. She tightened as his hand landed; it was hard and the surface of his palm was leathery and rough. He smacked her again and she cried out. Sparton tightened his grip and carried her around the ring, her naked sex exposed between the cheeks of her bottom, until another gladiator stepped forward. He was small but heavily built and he licked his hand before swinging it down onto Caristia's wriggling, upturned buttocks. There was a loud wet smack as it landed and again Caristia tensed in Sparton's vicelike grip. She threw out her legs and kicked, but it did not stop her being offered again, and when she was smacked a third time, and kicked even harder than before, it only increased the men's amusement and made them more keen to continue.

When they had all taken a turn Sparton carried her to the centre of the enclosure, bent down on one knee and laid her across it. He held her down easily, wedging his left elbow between her shoulder blades and pressing the outspread fingers of his hand into the dipping curve of the small of her back. She still kicked with undiminished energy, and as she flailed her legs the sunlight caught a glint of moisture between her thighs. Sparton smoothed his right hand across her reddened bottom then reached to the heavy leather belt that hung from his waist. He removed a short sword from a leather scabbard then pulled the scabbard itself from the metal clip that held it. It was almost the width of his hand and about the length of his forearm, made from carefully worked brown leather, sewn along its length both front and rear with a raised cross-stitch of leather lacing. He held it by the pointed tip, wrapping his large fingers around it and grasping it tightly. He flexed it and it bent only slightly, then he rubbed it against Caristia's buttocks in slow circling movements.

She responded instantly to its touch, its worn smoothness, its flatness, its potential. She stopped kicking, for a moment enthralled by the contact with the scabbard. Then, when it was removed, she waited spellbound, knowing what would happen, tensing in readiness, breathing in time with the potential contained in the nothingness that engulfed her.

Her orgasm began with the first spank. The flatness of the leather scabbard, the smooth contact, the width of its face and the slapping sound of its kiss, energized her body with an overflow of pleasure. As each slap landed on her taut skin, as each smack filled her ears she anticipated the next. As soon as the fire from one strike penetrated her body she desired the promise of what would follow. And, as each slap covered her bottom, the flesh of her cunt swelled more, moistened more, and this nectar, this sweet fuel stoked the fires of her orgasm. She relaxed less after each convulsive tightening of her body and, in the end, while the leather scabbard still fell with punishing blows, she was gripped by an overpowering, convulsive paroxysm. She tightened her buttocks together, increasing the redness that covered them, squeezing the swollen flesh of her cunt, driving the pain of pleasure throughout her body until it was, with jerking shudders, released. But it did not end, and as he continued spanking her, disciplining her, training her, each fresh blow released in her a new shiver of ecstasy and a fresh craving for more pain. Finally, still shaking with bliss and still lifting her buttocks to the cruel scabbard, she was dropped from his knee to the dusty ground.

As Caristia wiped the dust from her eyes the gladiators moved back and Bec was driven into the enclosure. She was blindfolded and her body was laced with chains. Her legs and arms were bare and she had been dressed in a tight-fitting black leather costume, pulled up high onto her hips and buckled on her shoulders. Holes were cut out for her breasts and they thrust prominently. The chains encircled her upper thighs, pulled between her legs, around her waist and between her breasts until they finished, padlocked at her neck. Her arms were tied behind her back and her forearms, bent at right angles, were chained together so that each hand touched the other elbow. She turned her head, as if looking around, and spat, strands of her black hair caught in her mouth. She kicked at the ground with her bare feet like a bull and the sun glinted on her toenails, painted a glossy red.

'Chain the little one as well!' shouted Sparton.

Men rushed forward and began lacing Caristia's naked body with heavy chain. Bec turned to the noise and ran over blindly. Several gladiators intercepted her but they struggled to bring to her to the ground and when, finally, they got her down another had to join them to help keep her under control. Caristia trembled at the sight of her enemy and felt weakened by her very presence. As the chains were bound around her the weight made her feel helpless and limp and she struggled to walk as they were both driven out of the arched gate and into the road outside.

Caristia and Bec emerged to the roar of the crowd which had gathered especially to see them. Bec twisted her shoulders from side to side, rattling the chains that bound her and making those nearest to her back away in fear. Caristia hung her head, ashamed to be seen like this, chained and naked and shaking with fear at what was going to happen. Men pushed around her, touching her hair, pulling it and making her cry out. Some of them felt her breasts and as many as could get close enough thrust their hands between her legs and felt the soft flesh of her slit. Some even managed to push their fingers between the velvety labia and penetrate the moist interior of her vagina.

As they were driven forward by large Nubians with whips men jeered at them, exposing themselves and lewdly pulling their cocks. One held his in front of Caristia's face when she fell to the ground, and pulling it frantically, sprayed his semen onto her parched lips. She licked at it and drew it into her mouth, enjoying its taste as though it made her forget the humiliation of being driven through the streets like a captive animal. Someone started spanking her buttocks to encourage her to get up. For a moment she felt peaceful as the hand smacked her, but as the crowd roared louder she knew it was an instruction to get to her feet rather than a delightful punishment for some disobedience or wrongdoing. Another hand joined the first, smacking her buttocks in unison, so she crawled to her feet and started again to struggle along the road.

They were both taunted all the way, Bec turning blindly to each poke or jeer and Caristia flinching and turning away from every mocking insult, keeping her eyes fixed firmly to the ground. They passed Rufo's house, and outside a brothel the owner rushed down and offered the guards escorting them a heavy wooden yoke with three holes, a large one in the centre and two smaller ones to the sides. The Nubians took it eagerly and made Caristia kneel down and have it fitted. They released her hands and pushed her head and hands through the holes before chaining her wrists again and leading the free ends to the iron collar around her neck. It was so heavy she had to be helped to her feet, and when she stood she could not hold herself upright and she swayed, bent slightly forward with her tangled blonde hair framing her plaintive face.

When they crossed the road which led to the Temple of Isis the procession stopped. Bec's chains were fed through an iron ring in the wall and she was pulled up tight against it. Her legs were manacled and the manacles were secured to a stake. She could hardly move, and although she struggled against her bonds, men now approached her without fear. They rubbed their cocks against her breasts and ejaculated wherever they wanted. One of them held his cock between the tops of her thighs as he finished, but as his semen was running down the insides of her legs she managed to pull one of the stakes free and clamped her legs together, trapping him and making him scream. It took six of them to free him. When they had secured the stake again the man insisted that she be punished, so they turned her around and bent her forward over a counter where drinks were sold. Her face was forced into one of the deep recesses where containers of oil were usually kept, and choking and gasping she was first whipped across the back with a short riding crop, before a leather flail, split into two separate strands, was laid across her bottom.

Caristia flinched each time the two thin strips of leather bit into Bec's muscular buttocks. They laced her skin with red stripes, some going down as far as the backs of her knees and others as high as the small of her back. Each time they landed Bec tightened her body but her response was as much a way of showing she could resist the pain as it was a reaction to the pain itself. Each man took a turn, but they could not make her shriek or cry out and, in the end, they tired of her and turned their attentions to Caristia.

She struggled against them as they hauled her onto the counter alongside Bec, and she cried out as, still with the yoke securing her head and hands, they tied her down against the cold marble top. She begged them to let her go but her pleas for mercy and weak attempts at escape did nothing to stop them doing as they wished. The split leather lashed down across her buttocks and she yelled out pitifully. Her cries delighted the men and they pushed at each other to take their turn. The slapping sound filled her ears as, with each blow, the split leather smacked her twice in quick succession. The first pain, from the leading flail, filled her and the second, following close behind, drove her to overflowing. The sense of captivity and the deep humiliation of public exposure saturated her with anxiety, but each time the first smack smarted her stinging bottom, each time the second stung her more than she could ever imagine, she could do nothing but lift her bottom to meet it. The pain was like a magnet, drawing her towards it, causing her to raise her buttocks and open them and expose her slit. She flinched and gasped but still she lifted herself higher and made her flesh more available. The pain was ecstasy and she opened herself as much as possible, exposing herself to more.

She rode the flailing strap, rising like a tide against its flow of pain and dipping only to recover enough tension to meet it again, pushing herself against each blow, lifting herself as it drew away. She gripped her hands into fists as wave after wave of pleasure coursed through her like a flooding river of ecstasy. She dropped forward when they had finished with her, her elbows dipping below the yoke, her head hanging loosely through the hole at its centre. She was depleted, exhausted, finished as she hung there, gasping for air.

She did not know whether her orgasms were still gripping her or whether she was jerking with pain when they lifted her away from the counter and again set her to march along the cobbled street. She licked her lips and focused her bleary eyes. She stumbled against Bec, who turned and spat viciously at her like a startled snake. Bec kept turning her head from side to side, listening, trying to locate her prey, and as Caristia swung away and ducked another glob of spit, she saw the bare rage that lurked within her animal-like opponent.

As they passed below the balcony of the Happy Phoenix, pots of wine were emptied down onto them and men and women rushed up and licked it from them. Caristia tasted the red wine on her lips as it ran down her face, over her breasts and down between her legs. She felt its warmth against the flesh of her sex, which as well as her humiliating exposure to the crowd, caused her own moisture to flow. She gasped as a young woman knelt in front of her and clutched the backs of her thighs so she could squeeze her face tightly between her thighs. The woman probed her tongue against the warm, wine-soaked sex lips and lapped eagerly, running the tip along the wet valley, peeling the lips apart and delving into the exposed warmth of hidden flesh. Two men took hold of the yoke and lifted so that the young woman could press her tongue deeper. Caristia hung there, suspended by her wrists and neck as the female lifted Caristia's legs and draped them over her shoulders so she was exposed fully for her relish.

Caristia rose and fell with the lapping tongue, urging it deeper, moving sideways first so that it ran smoothly along the soft edges then dropping down to enjoy the penetration as its tip squirmed inside her. She lifted her head in rapture as her clitoris swelled against the licking tongue and her joy, together with the heat of contact, made it throb and enlarge even more until it pressed like a pulsating bud against the source of its pleasure. The men holding the yoke lowered it, bending her so that her buttocks were lifted, then still with the young woman moaning and slurping between her thighs, another woman started spanking her with a leather strop.

The blows were heavy and the strap lashed around Caristia's hips, but the pain coupled with the delving tongue caused her to yell out loud in a fit of ecstasy. She screamed each time the strap landed, each time she felt it burning her skin, reddening her and lacing her with pain. But it was not a response to her suffering; it was a scream of passion, of submission to her own unbridled gratification. More wine was thrown over her and it ran through her hair, down her back and cooled her bottom. The slapping of the strop was louder against her wet skin and the slurping of the woman's tongue was more pronounced, and when Caristia was doused again she howled as her orgasm ripped through her body in an eruption of bliss.

The Nubian guards came into the crowd and pushed the women away. They drove the two captives on, Caristia trudging under the weight of the yoke, dripping with red wine and jerking with the last twitches of her ecstasy. Bec still spitting and blindly lurching at anything she heard.

They were forced into a low tunnel that entered the side of the Amphitheatre and made to wait, kneeling on the sandy ground, behind a heavy grill that led onto the arena. Caristia stared through it and saw her mistress in a ringside box almost within touching distance.

Arria Sulla pulled herself eagerly to the front of the box. Fronto sat beside her, and dressed in a long robe and untethered, Innocenti sat by his side. When Caristia saw her she felt a wave of nerves rise in her stomach as an anxious concern flowed through her. But Innocenti's pale skin looked radiant and her dark eyes flashed in the flickering light of the torches that surrounded the arena. Her hair had been done up in pigtails and the tied ends were bent vertically like small horns. She looked youthfully elegant and at ease, and she punched Fronto playfully in the arm as he played with one of her pigtails. Caristia screwed up her eyes, unsure of what she was seeing, confused by the sight of the delicate slavegirl apparently at ease in the company of her master and mistress. She looked away, and in a smaller box on the opposite side of the arena Rufo sat, with Magnus standing behind him. Rufo nodded to Fronto, and when he did not get an acknowledgment he stroked his hair back as though his nod had been caused by a fallen curl.

Half naked male slaves brought in heavy boards and began erecting two adjoining corrals. They built up the boards to just above head height, then strung a wire mesh netting across the tops before drawing a long flat board across each enclosure to act as a walkway. Other men, all naked, ran around the edges lighting torches and propping them up high on lances. Above each of the corrals a heavy bell was suspended from a rope drawn down from a timber jib, itself part of the partial roofing system of the high-sided Amphitheatre. Several large X-shaped crucifixes were dragged in and propped into readymade holes in the ground. Caristia's stomach churned with fear as she saw them.

'Very well, madam,' said Fronto, edging himself to the front of the box and patting his thigh for Innocenti to move closer to him. 'Let us be clear about the "special" rules you have promised. Although, I have to say, the rules of gladiatorial combat are usually straightforward and I cannot imagine what you have in mind.'

Arria Sulla smiled and leant over to him.

'You did promise to accept my rules, did you not?'

'Yes madam. State them so we may proceed.'

'Very well. It is easy, my dear Lucretius Fronto. Each of our contestants will be put into one of the enclosures that have been erected to my special instructions. Then,' she smiled, pausing long enough to detect Fronto's impatience, 'then, each enclosure will be filled with men I have chosen especially for their sexual prowess. Each of our gladiators must remain in the enclosure and satisfy all the men. If either one of them tries to escape by seeking sanctuary outside the enclosure, or cannot continue to satisfy their lovers' demands, then she will be the loser. Either an exhausted contestant will climb up and ring the bell as a sign of her defeat, or the bell will be tolled by a dissatisfied paramour. Whichever is the case, at the toll of the bell we will know the loser and we will applaud our victor.'

Fronto scowled, and for a moment pursed his lips as he prepared to challenge Arria Sulla's rules for the contest, then tossing his head back nonchalantly he succumbed to good humour and smiled broadly.

'It is agreed! A marvellous idea!' he shouted. 'Madam, you have a talent for the exciting. Now, we need an enthusiastic crowd. Let us warm up their appetite.' He waved to the Nubians who guarded the entrance gate. 'Bring on the entertainment so that when our gladiators enter the ring they will be given a hearty welcome.'

A fanfare sounded and Caristia watched from behind the grill as Minimus and his troop bounded into the arena. The crowd cheered as the agile dwarf ran around the edges of the barriers which kept the crowd back, exposing his huge cock and letting any women close enough feel it or even suck it. A huddled group of freshly imported slave women were driven in by black slaves with spears. They shrank back as the crowd shouted and taunted them. Two were pulled free of the cowering group and tied onto the X-shaped crosses fixed into the ground. Their mouths were gagged and they were whipped. Their breasts became quickly marked with jagged red lines, then as they began to slump under the strain of their painful punishment they were turned around and men from the crowd came down and took turns spanking them. The women wailed in agony and the men competed with each other to see who could make their victims cry out the loudest. The men's laughter and the women's cries mixed together with the cheers of the crowd in a hellish chaos of anguish and pleasure.

The women were untied and turned upside down on the crosses. They were spanked again but the men could not resist and most of them plunged fingers between the slaves' legs or thrust their faces against them. One of the women huddling by the entrance tunnel was spread-eagled and tied to a cart wheel with heavy rope. Her naked body was doused in oil and then the wheel was bowled from one side of the arena to the other. The crowd threw down food at her as she spun across the arena and, when the wheel toppled, several men leapt down and plunged their cocks one after the other into her sex and mouth. As the crowd roared the woman was released, tied to ropes by the heels, then dragged through the dusty arena by two Nubian slaves. She was hauled up by her ankles on the end of a long pole and the two Nubians stretched the pole out over the crowd and passed the woman over their heads. They struggled to keep the pole in the air as men in the crowd lurched at the woman, grabbing her hair and trying to reach her breasts. Two women climbed down into the arena and tore at their own clothes until only tattered rags hung about their waists. They started wrestling each other, rolling in the dust as they clawed at the final remnants of clothing and pulled at each other's hair. Nubian slaves were sent to separate and drag them away, but even as they were pulled out through the exit tunnel they continued to fight and claw at each other in an uncontrollable frenzy. As they were driven into a large cage at the rear of the tunnel they clasped their legs around the Nubians' hips and forced themselves down onto their hard cocks.

Slaves attached a collar first to Caristia's neck, then to Bec's. Two lines of girls, naked except for coronets of white flowers in their hair, lined up in front of them. Other slaves clipped a rope into each of the collars and then the ropes were pulled out and draped over the shoulders of the two lines of waiting girls. The girls pulled and both women fell forward, Caristia because she was struggling to carry the weight of the heavy yoke, and Bec because she could not see. Another fanfare was sounded, the grill that separated Caristia and Bec from the arena was lifted, and the two were hauled in.

Slaves with whips drove them from behind, and slowly they were positioned in front of the boards which led across the separate enclosures from which the metal nets had now been peeled back. The yoke was removed from Caristia and she was lifted up onto the board by the Nubians. Other slaves pushed her forward, and unable to resist them she walked along the board nervously, then just as she reached the centre they tipped it and she fell into the enclosure. They swept the netting across quickly, trapping her inside, and she clawed up at it like a captured animal. They then used poles with rings to hold Bec by the neck and guide her up onto the boards, then keeping her balanced in the centre, one of them climbed up and released her chains. As soon as she was free of her bonds they let go of the poles and tipped her into the enclosure too. She fell on her back, and still with the poles extending from her neck she ripped the blindfold from her eyes. She looked around savagely as the netting was drawn quickly over the top of the enclosure, and frustrated by her captivity she began running against the boards that surrounded her, charging and crashing into them noisily with her shoulders.

Arria Sulla signalled to the Nubians at the entrance tunnel and they opened the gates to two large cages drawn by six horses. Each cage was filled with men. Some were covered in animal skins and roared and clawed as if they were themselves animals. Some were dressed as warriors and carried spears or swords, some wore masks and black leather tunics and wielded whips, and others were black naked savages with huge headdresses and rings in their noses. The crowd howled its approval as the cages were paraded around the arena, until finally they were drawn up alongside the enclosures that imprisoned Caristia and Bec. Nubians clambered on top of the cages and stood ready to lift the doors and temporarily remove some of the boards that would release the men into the two enclosures - the masked men in leather tunics and those in animal skins into Caristia's, and the warriors and naked savages into Bec's.

Fronto stood up and held his arms high. The crowd roared, then knowing their pleasure awaited a signal from one of the patrician class, they quietened until there was not a sound.

'Now,' said Fronto triumphantly, 'on this twenty-fourth day of the month of Augustus, let this special contest begin!'

Chapter 12
The contest

The Nubians on top of the cages pulled up the doors and the boards of the enclosures then quickly jumped down and ran to the sides of the arena. There was a moment when nothing happened, even Bec stood still and stared at the opening into the cage, then as if the doors to hell itself had been opened, there was pandemonium.

The first ones to rush towards their quarry were the men in animal skins. But they had hardly moved, holding their hands up like claws and snarling loudly before the others followed. The men in skins chased Caristia around the enclosure while the masked men stood around the edges and whipped her whenever she came close enough to them. She heard the crashes of swords and yelling in the other corral, but she could not see over the boards that penned her in. One of the men, an African wearing a lion skin with the open-jawed head as his headdress, grabbed her by the waist and brought her to the ground. She managed to wriggle away but he grabbed her ankles, pinned her fast and would not let go. Another held her by the shoulders and a third grasped her hair.

They pulled her over onto her back, pawing at her with their hands as though they were animals taunting their prey. Suddenly one of them lunged at her, gripping one of her nipples between his teeth and grasping her sex in his hand. She gasped as he pinched her labia, squeezing them between his fingers and digging his nails into their exposed softness. Another man, a buffalo skin secured at his neck by its heavy front legs and its horned, wide-eyed head fixed low over his eyes, knelt across her shoulders, facing her feet, and lowered his balls over her face. They swung heavily against her mouth as he squeezed her cheeks and forced her lips open. She let out a squeal and with her labia pinched and her nipple being bitten, she was seized with a flood of pain and fear.

The next she knew they threw her onto her front, holding her shoulders to the ground and lifting her bottom. They parted her legs wide and she felt the lion's mane tickling the insides of her thighs as the man wearing it licked up the length of her slit, then drove his tongue into her anus. She felt it inside her rectum as the tip probed and explored. She clawed at the ground, gripping the sand and forcing it between her fingers as he pulled away and placed the bulbous tip of his rigid cock against the opening. He pushed it in without stopping, all the way to the root, filling her rear passage, making her scream out and at the same time, starting the flow of her own unstoppable orgasm.

As he finished inside her rear, saturating her with his copious flow of semen, the men in the leather tunics and masks moved in and hauled her to the boards at the side of the enclosure. She did not want to release the cock from her anus, she wanted to squeeze it until all his semen was inside her, and when they pulled her away she felt suddenly empty and in need of filling again. She escaped from the masked men and ran to the centre of the enclosure and bent on all fours, lifting her bottom, inviting the men in animal skins to fill it, to drive their cocks into it, to drench her with their heat. One of the masked men snapped his whip and its tattered end flicked across her buttocks. It was only a glance but it burned her sharply, but although she flinched she did not pull away nor hold back from what she wanted, and she dropped her shoulders lower, opened her thighs slightly and lifted her bottom even higher. The whip cracked again, a sudden burning snap, and she felt its sting but again she pushed her shoulders down and lifted her buttocks. Another crack and another stinging pain but she opened her legs wider, revealing her sex, and the next one that struck caught her exposed labia.

She yelled out with each fiery crack of the whip, but the pain only encouraged her to want more so she rolled over on her back, lifted her legs and let them whip between her legs. Even as the whips laced her flesh, as the sound of pain filled her ears, she heard the crowd roaring and, as each whipping snap landed against her flesh she heard their baying rise to a fresh crescendo. The roaring crowd, the exposure and the delectable pain drew an orgasm from her that reached every nerve, every sense and every corner of her ecstatic body. Each movement was a signal for it to flow more, each flinch a flare that relit the flames that scorched her. When one of the animal men knelt between her legs and drove his cock again into her anus, the surge of her orgasm was like the flow of a drowning tide and she howled as if once beneath this sea of pleasure she might never breathe again.

They lifted her up onto the boards so she could see over the side. Bec was fighting with the savages. They surrounded her in a circle, wary of her yet at the same time aware that they outnumbered her. Caristia watched them pinning her to the ground, stripping her leather costume away, exposing her black pubic hair and revealing her rounded breasts. Then she watched them bending her over one of their backs and beating her with a leather belt. The warriors joined in, tying her with leather thongs and holding her against the enclosure wall to be spanked. Caristia watched Bec's buttocks reddening and she saw that no matter what they did to her she would never show that she was suffering.

Caristia wanted spanking like Bec. She wanted the feel of a hand across her bottom, but unlike Bec she wanted to scream. She wanted to yell each time the hand came down on her skin; she wanted to expel her pain and let it mix with the thrill. The hands holding her slackened for a moment and she wriggled free. The man in the lion skin fell back onto the ground, the lion's head falling low on his face and the skin folding around his hips. His cock, hard and throbbing, stuck up between the folds of the skin and, when Caristia saw it she straddled him and dropped down onto it. She threw herself forward, lifting her buttocks and exposing them for punishment. One of the masked men dropped his whip and bent down to her. He held his hand across the taut skin of her bottom, then when she tensed and squeezed down onto the cock inside her, he lifted his hand away and brought it down with all his force.

The smack was so hard that the breath was knocked from her in a sudden explosion of air. She reared back but as soon as she moved she felt the hardness of the cock inside her, and still arching her back she drove herself further down onto it. She lifted her bottom again and the next smack fell immediately. It stung so deeply, penetrated her body with tongues of fire, but the pain only incensed her. It only fed her passion and she pulled herself up and down the stiff cock, wriggling from side to side, tightening herself on it until, squeezing her eyes tightly together in frustrated anticipation, the next smack struck. Again and again the hand spanked her bottom, reddening it, setting it on fire and again and again she rose to meet it, squeezing the cock inside her cunt and yelling with desire and suffering. She took it all, and when at last she felt the surge of hot semen inside her she climbed off the man and another took his place. The spanking continued, each strike filling her with pain but the pain only driving her to want more.

As she climbed from the third man she was lifted and draped again against the boards of the enclosure. She hung her head over the edge, watching her enemy as the spanking continued, as the fire of passion kept burning. Bec had not given in and her resistance only angered her antagonists. They stalked her in a circle, spitting their resentment and kicking dust into her face, jabbing at her with their spears or lurching at her savagely. Suddenly, acting together out of some intuition, they flung themselves at her and wrestled her to the ground. Two of them stood over her and pulled at their stiff cocks until their seed erupted. It dribbled into her mouth and she spat it out, but even though she shook her head vigorously she could not stop it running into her nostrils and her eyes. One of the warriors lifted his sword and sliced at the wire netting that covered the enclosure. It tore into jagged strips and he clambered up through it and onto the board that stretched across the width of the pen. Caristia saw what he was going to do and watched him, balancing on the board and reaching up high towards the hanging bell. She reared back against the heavy spanking, lifting her face up into the night sky, and like a victorious animal she yelled at the top of her voice as the man grabbed hold of the rope that hung from the clanger and rang it as a frantic signal of Bec's defeat.

Caristia fell back to the ground, stretching her arms out wide and spreading her hands flat in the dirt. The Amphitheatre filled with the clamorous roar of the crowd. It was like a storm, a heavy roll of thunder. Caristia felt it under her back, reverberating like an explosion or the beating of a heavy drum. Then she felt something different. There was a heavy rumble beneath her, shuddering against her shoulder blades, coming from somewhere deep. She felt it against the palms of her hands, then she felt her whole body moving as it shook the very fabric of the earth. It was as if the world was breaking in half.

Everything stopped, the crowd went silent, no one knew what was happening, what to expect next. Some even thought their senses were deceiving them. But as they turned to each other with worried faces, they realised they had not been mistaken. It happened again, another heavy rumble, this time stronger, more intense, as if the planet's core was preparing to explode. It was like the low growl of a suffering dragon, woken by a terrifying pain, then as if its suffering had become unbearable the tortured beast was letting out a snarling, deafening roar. The ground shook in long, resounding booms. It felt as though they would never stop, and the dark sky was lit up by a billow of rolling flames erupting from the crater of the bursting Vesuvius. A column of flame rose into the sky, lighting it from beneath, picking out the dark clouds which hung above the waking monster. Then, as if this was not enough, the whole broad base of the crater lifted into the sky as though plucked from the earth by a god. The mountain opened down its flank as it was ripped apart and the crater which had been torn from its root was atomized into a storm of airborne ash and fire.

Caristia ran to the edge of the enclosure and clambered up the sides of the boards. She pressed against the metal meshing and watched as Bec was confronted by a crowd running in through the broken down entrance. Bec struggled against the flood of men in the enclosure as they poured in through the opened gate. They had seen her overcome by the caged gladiators and now, terrified and confused by the fire-filled sky and deafened by the roaring volcano, could think of nothing else other than taking pleasure for themselves. Bec could not stand against them, it was impossible, there were too many and she buckled under their weight and fell to the ground.

Caristia could not bear to see her subjected to the savagery of the desperate men. Even though she was her enemy, she admired her prowess and strength, and without thinking about the consequences she squeezed between the tops of the boards and the netting and dropped into the other enclosure. She tried to fight her way through the seething mob, guided by Bec's fading cries, but it was hopeless, she could not get to her... and then she saw Bec's hand stretching out of the churning crowd and managed to get close enough to grab it.

'Remember me,' Bec said, struggling to speak under the pressure of the bodies engulfing her. 'Remember Bec, the daughter of Thorkell the Dane...'

Caristia let go of the weakening hand and it disappeared beneath the panicking throng. Caristia turned to push her way back but straightaway she saw she could not escape either; the crowd were going wild and they did not care who they attacked. She struck out at them, desperate to get away from their grabbing hands, but she fell to the ground coughing and choking in the whipped up dust storm of fear. The crowd's feet were all around her and she feared being trampled, then just as she was giving up all hope a powerful black arm swept down and lifted her by the waist.

Magnus held her high, pushing the crowd aside, kicking them, punching them, fighting for his prize. He was too powerful for any of them and they fell aside like dolls as he ran, carrying Caristia, out of the exit tunnel and into the cobbled street.

'Magnus,' she said breathlessly, as she lay in his arms, 'I must find Drusus, Fronto's slave. Magnus, I must find him.'

'I know where he is,' said Magnus, looking around at the panicking crowds running amok in the streets. 'I will take you to him.'

Magnus ran through the streets with Caristia in his arms. She felt the strength of his muscular arms around her and, even surrounded by the fiery sky and the roaring waves of noise that spewed from the volcano, she felt a sense of safety in his powerful grip. As they reached the Gymnasium a dust of hot ash began falling from the sky. People in the street held out their hands to catch it, sniffed at it and pawed at it with their fingers, as if it was a source of amusement, as if it was no threat.

In the centre of the open colonnaded training square of the Gymnasium Drusus hung tethered against a stake. Caristia wriggled from Magnus's arms and ran towards him, but the young men who trained there, pretending that the ash-spewing mountain which overshadowed them was somehow subordinate to their youthful powers, intercepted her and surrounded her in a jeering ring. She looked into their eyes and although she saw some fear reflected in the red shimmering light cast by the volcano, she also saw a stubborn, juvenile refusal to accept their obvious fate. Like the crowd who had attacked and overcome Bec, they too seemed to think that worldly pleasures would somehow rid them of the terrors which threatened to extinguish their lives altogether.

Caristia dodged from side to side, hoping to break their ranks and run between them, but it only amused them. Magnus stepped in front of her, but he was no match for them either. They were fit, trained for combat and outnumbered him, and quickly they brought him down and bound him by the wrists and ankles. Caristia's eyes filled with tears when she saw him lying helpless on the ground. She wanted to do something to help him, but she did not know what and all she could think of as a shimmering covering of ash slowly coated the Nubian's bound body, was Drusus, and how to get him free.

'This is the little slave who likes a spanking,' shouted a young blond man wearing only tight trunks. 'Fronto has talked about her. Apparently her thirst for pleasure is unquenchable.'

They all laughed as they gathered around her.

'Bring her over to the vaulting horse,' shouted another. 'There can be nothing better to secure a slave who has a desire for spanking.'

Caristia looked back at Magnus, bound by the hands and feet and lying on the ash covered ground. His red eyes looked away, as if he felt guilty for failing to protect her, and he lay back and opened his mouth, inviting the volcano to fill him with its fatal heat and take away his shame.

Caristia reached towards him but the young men dragged her away, pulling her into the middle of the training area at the centre of the colonnaded square. The clouds darkened overhead as heaving billows of ash-laden smoke filled the crimson sky, and the marble columns that surrounded the square were lit red like giant torches.

'Here,' shouted one of the young men. 'Tie her to the top. Bend her over so that her buttocks are exposed fully to the reddening sky and the spanking she is going to get.'

Two of them lifted her up and bent her over the side of the vaulting horse.

She was draped across the suede leather top and her hands stretched around it until they reached her ankles on the other side. They bound them together with some used bandages and secured the ends to the feet of the timber construction. Caristia's blonde hair trailed down in a tangle as she stared underneath the horse. Everything looked red, everything looked on fire, everywhere looked like hell. Not far away she could see Drusus, hanging in his bonds, looking towards her helplessly, unable to save her, forced to watch her suffering. The sight of him made her think again of the escape he had promised, and under the vermilion turmoil of the boiling sky she was filled with a deep sense of despair.

The young men argued about who would be first and they pushed each other until one was chosen. He stood behind Caristia and circled her bottom with his hand. It was a young hand, soft and strong, and his touch was light. It tingled her skin and the image of Drusus faded in her mind as she waited for the young man to lift his hand away and sweep it down for the first delightful smack. The others urged him to get on with it as he continued to feel her buttocks, but he would not be rushed and, even as another distant explosion came from the erupting volcano, he waited. Caristia tightened her buttocks slightly, but she knew she must not respond too much; his gentle touch was not expecting a response, and surrounded by the hellish fire of impending doom, she closed her eyes and lingered under his delicate control.

She did not feel him lift his hand away, his touch had been so light, but she heard it cutting the air as he brought it down and the sound of its sharp smack filled her ears before the pain that followed it entered her mind. It was hard and sharp and smarted deeply, but again, before she had fully absorbed it, he circled her bottom with his hand, calming her, forcing her to wait. Again she closed her eyes before he lifted away and again she was only warned of the approach of pain by the swishing of his fingers through the air as he swept his hand down for a second time.

Another explosion from the volcano sounded only like a faint rumble of thunder to Caristia as the young man continued spanking her. She felt punished and yet she did not know what for, and she felt caressed even though the caresses brought pain. She knew her bottom lifted to his smarting smacks and she knew he could see her cunt squeezed tightly at the base of her buttocks, where they joined her thighs. When she thought of these things she felt a running heat inside the swelling flesh of her exposed slit. The smacks kept coming; solid, hard and sharp, rhythmic, paced, dispassionate. Caristia rose to each one more than the one before, and with each increase in pain she felt the approaching closeness of her orgasm. She opened her eyes for a moment and saw the redness of hell descending on the earth, then as the young man quickened his smacks she held her breath, bit her lip and let her orgasm seize her.

He kept spanking her until the last convulsion of her orgasm had passed, then stepped back and let another take his place. This one was harder, quicker and sent sharp stings through her sensitized buttocks but now it did not matter; she only wanted the feel of a hand on her bottom. She did not care how hard it was, how quick, how punishing, as long as it kept coming. As long as it thrashed her until another convulsion of ecstasy was drawn from her heaving body. She pulled her bound wrists against her ankles to increase the tension across her buttocks and, as the pace of the hand built to a rapid crescendo she finished again, groaning first then letting it go in a sudden screech of pleasure.

They all took their turn, spanking her first with their hands then with a cane, and her buttocks, at first smudged with redness from their palms were soon laced with sharp red lines from the rod. She rode it all, lifting herself to each smack as it came down, absorbing the heat dispensed to her from the slashing cane, revelling in the perfection of pain that coursed through her.

They cut her free and laid her on her back along the top of the leather-covered vaulting horse. Her legs fell loosely at the sides, stretching the muscles in her thighs, accentuating her hipbones. Her sex was pulled under the tension, lengthened by the strain of being stretched, the lips squeezed together into a neat oval. Her breasts were flattened against her chest, her nipples hard and her arms hung down limply, emphasising her shoulders. Her head hung back and her blonde hair draped, exposing her small ears and high-boned cheeks. She stared up into the angry red sky, completely vulnerable.

The young men fought with each other to be first to get on top of her. In the end one of them knelt between her thighs and held his throbbing cock in his hands. He pressed the glans against the tight slit and moved it sideways until he opened it. The moisture from within her flesh ran across the tip of his cock, making it shine red in the fiery light of the tormented sky. He leant forward and drove it into her, sinking it to the root in one long push. He thrust at her, and with each strong stroke she lifted her legs a little higher, first to the sides of his thighs, then his hips, his waist and finally she brought them up as high as she could and wrapped them around his neck. He kept thrusting his cock into her, then as he grasped her stretched buttocks in his hands she reared up and he finished deep inside her jerking body. She clung to him as he finished, sucking every drop of semen from him, drawing it out as if it was her last act. The others took her in the same way and she reared up on every one, letting the convulsions of her orgasms run into one another, allowing her pleasure to join into a single stream of blissful ecstasy.

Two of them pushed their cocks into her mouth and she sucked both as they finished at the same time, but increasingly they became aware of the ever-reddening sky and the ash falling about them. Some of them pulled on tunics but most left naked, heading for the exit of the town and the turmoil that lay beyond the enclosure of the Gymnasium. Caristia leant against the vaulting horse, breathing hard, still feeling the heat of pleasure inside her semen-filled cunt. She draped her arms over the top and pushed her bottom out, hoping that one of the young men would return and take advantage of her again, but they had all gone.

Another explosion roared from the bowels of the volcano and, as if woken from a reverie, Caristia turned to Drusus, still hanging where he had been tied. She ran to him and struggled to free him. When she finally managed to he held her in his arms and looked up into the sky.

'We must hurry,' he said, picking up a discarded tunic and wrapping it around her as protection against the falling ash. 'If we can only get to the sea I know we will be safe.' They ran past Magnus, and Caristia held back and tried to bend down to him. Drusus pulled her away and shook his head. 'It is too late for him,' he said breathlessly. 'But we still have a chance.'

He pulled her out into the street and back into the panicking crowd that thronged in a confused melee of fear and helpless terror.

Chapter 13
Death on the road to Stablae

Hand in hand, Caristia and Drusus ran along the cinder-strewn road towards the small coastal town of Stablae. It was as though they were inside a vast cauldron, coughing in the choking smoke, their feet burning on the fiery ash as it boiled around them. Suddenly Caristia stopped, frightened by the sight of two women tied to X-shaped crosses by the roadside. They were both naked, their hair sticking in straggling strands to their sweating faces, their mouths covered by leather gags, their arms pinned outwards and upwards and their legs widespread. Their wrists were bound tightly to the upper beams of the outward pointing timbers and their ankles were secured with leather thongs so that their feet were well clear of the ground. Their eyes, glowing with the fire from the sky, made them look as if they were burning from within their tortured bodies. Several soldiers taunted them, prodding with lances or pushing their faces between the terrified women's legs. The women flung their heads from side to side, as if trying to show they were resisting their torturers but, by their desperate actions, only proving their helpless captivity. A little further on Caristia and Drusus came across a group of men spanking a girl. Her naked body was passed from one to the other as each took turns in draping her slight form across their knees. She screamed in panic, struggling to escape their clutches, to run to the sea and hopefully find safety, but it was a pointless hope. Her upturned bottom, reddened by their hands and the light of the fiery mountain of Vesuvius, would provide the final pleasure for the men and the final pain for their victim.

At last Caristia and Drusus made it to Stablae, and barely in time. The deafening roar of the volcano had increased, its smoking plume rising ever higher into the darkened sky. The shower of hot ash, only a drizzle when they had left Pompeii, was now a full blown storm of fire.

'Drusus,' she choked, 'are we safe? Tell me we are safe.'

Drusus looked exhausted but did not show Caristia his fear.

'We are nearly at the shore,' he said. 'There we will be safe. Yes, we will find a boat and be safe. Soon, my sweet, we will be safe with the Arabs of the African desert.'

As they ran down the stony shore she saw just one small boat, surrounded by an angry crowd. The wretched mob fought each other in the hope of claiming a place in the already overburdened boat, which wallowed in the flat red swell.

'We are going to die,' she said, filled with despair. 'We will not be able to escape.'

'We will, my sweet,' he said, grabbing her and running towards the crimson waves. 'Just a little further.'

He pulled her into the crowd and she was consumed, as if by a massive swarm of bees desperate to surround their queen. Hands caught hold of her, pulling her in all directions, grasping her breasts, her cunt, her hair, her lips, and she was filled with panic.

'Drusus!' she screamed, unable to see him any more. 'Drusus!' she called hopelessly. 'Where are you?'

Drusus fought blindly with the wretched rabble, throwing himself towards Caristia's weakening voice, kicking at everyone around them, biting, anything to keep her from their grabbing hands. He gathered her up and managed to tear her away, and for that one moment, as she stared into his eyes, she felt free. It was as though at last they had escaped and were, on that reddened, violent shore, liberated from the tyranny of their cruel masters. But it was only for a moment.

The horde descended on them with renewed vigour, panic-stricken by their own fear of death, and even though Drusus still managed to hold Caristia high above them, he took the full force of their anger. He pitted himself with all his strength against the mass, but he sank slowly and irrevocably beneath their overwhelming power. She sensed his strength waning as still he struggled to carry her nearer the fragile boat, then with one final effort he flung her towards it. Already filled to the brim with fear-filled passengers, it was now being pushed out into the beckoning sanctuary of the sea.

As she was thrown down in the bottom of the boat she lost sight of Drusus. The last she saw of him was struggling beneath the feet of the angry mob, red ash billowing around him, as if he was being dragged down into hell by Satan's acolytes. She turned her face away, unable to face his suffering, and in the front of the boat, sucking avidly on a large cock as it drenched her face with semen, was Innocenti. Caristia's eyes widened, then as the glowing redness of a fresh eruption coloured everything with a deep crimson blush, she saw the man kneeling above the frail girl was Fronto. The boat lurched and she was thrown forward against the naked Innocenti. Her skin felt smooth and Caristia's nostrils filled with her soft fragrance. She looked up at Innocenti's face, pure and delicate, her upturned pigtails neatly braided at the sides of her head.

'Innocenti!' Caristia shouted. 'You are safe, but why...?' She wanted to ask what was going on. Why was Fronto, a cruel master who had subjected the girl to so much suffering now the subject of her passion? But she already knew the answer. It was written on Innocenti's eager, semen-soaked face, and on Fronto's glare of arrogant complicity. Innocenti did not reply, but encircling Fronto's pulsating cock with her delicate fingers she lapped at its tip, drinking everything that came from it.

'She is my wife,' announced Fronto, over the thunderous din of the eruption. 'I hope you didn't think she was a slave like you. But of course, she plays her part so well, her desire to suffer the punishment of slaves is so great, how could you know. How amusing. Yes, she is my wife, my little pleasure-seeking wife. It is one of her games. Does she not play her part to the full, little slave?'

Innocenti drew away for a moment, smiled, then again took his rigid cock into her open mouth and sucked. Her eyes closed as she swallowed it down and Caristia knew from the hollow tingling that filled her body the deep humiliation of intractable deceit.

Caristia, her world overturned and filled with blind panic, struggled to escape, to run back to the shore and find Drusus. But it was hopeless; the men in the boat fell on her like a pack of wolves, first tearing off her charred clothes then bending her over the central thwart and tying her tightly. They bound her wrists and ankles to each other so that her legs were bent wide at the knees and her buttocks were open. Her naked sex was fully exposed, its fleshy shape outlined by the red light in the sky. Fronto looked down at her as he stroked Innocenti's dark pigtails.

The men crowded around Caristia, seized with the panic of a final act, knowing their end was coming, desperate to fill their remaining life with action. Punishing her would be their last act, their last chance to obtain pleasure in the living world. She would be the object of all their pent-up passion, of everything they had ever desired. This subjugated form, this captive victim would be spanked by them all, then when the flesh of her cunt was swollen and heated and moist with passion, she would perform all their wishes. Then, when they were satiated, she would take their cocks and drink their semen. Caristia would satisfy them all before they were overcome, either with the fire or the fumes or the falling ash. She would bend for them in every way they imagined, fold herself forward and expose her bottom to them in all the ways they had ever wished. She would tighten the cheeks of her buttocks when they smacked her and would relax them between their blows so that they could see the perfect shape of her cunt as its soft flesh squeezed between her thighs. She would let them see the way it tightened again, anticipating the moment of contact, just before the flat of a hand landed in another punishing spank. She would lift her buttocks for them, imploring them to spank her harder, inviting them to use her in every way that pleased them. She would get down on all fours, dropping her forearms flat against the slopping wet boards of the crowded boat, submitting to them completely. And the end, the sound of their smacking hands reddening her bottom, already painted crimson by the fiery sky, would drown out the roar of the erupting volcano. The terror of the falling ash and the scorching heat of the choking air would be replaced with the flow of pleasure running from her swollen, moistened cunt.

The Diaries of Syra Bond

I felt the driver's fingers slip beneath the waist of my panties, lifting it away from my skin and peeling them down over my buttocks. He used both hands to expose my bottom, little by little. I relished the cool caress of the evening air against my nakedness. He drew the panties down my thighs, twisted the material and wedged it just above my knees before letting it go. My nipples hardened against my blouse and I swallowed hard as my mouth went dry with anticipation.

Imprisoned by a perverted captor, research student, Syra, is forced to write about the sexual misadventures that led to her captivity. She tells in explicit detail - and under constant censure and threat of punishment - how, in the heat if a long Spanish summer her cruel master, Galen, as part of an experiment in control, trains her to complete obedience. She recalls how she fulfils his every wish as, with a mixture of mental control and chastisement, he takes her to the limits of obedience where everything, real and imaginary, becomes part of the sexual world he contrives for her.

Syra's exposure to Galen's cruelty serves only to increase her desire for satisfaction from humiliation. But even though she submits to everything she is told - and there seems nothing that limits her desire for degradation - the final outcome proves to be an ultimate and unforeseen humiliation that sets the scene for the rest of her life.

Available to order as a paperback from AMAZON

www.ingramcontent.com/pod-product-compliance
Lightning Source LLC
Chambersburg PA
CBHW070758120626

46557CB00002B/652